Sebastian

Bowen Boys Book 5

By

KATHI S. BARTON

WCP

World Castle Publishing, LLC
Pensacola, Florida

Copyright © Kathi S. Barton 2014
Print ISBN: 9781629891071
eBook ISBN: 9781629891088
First Edition World Castle Publishing, LLC, June 13, 2014
http://www.worldcastlepublishing.com

Licensing Notes

Cover: Karen Fuller
Editor: Eric Johnston
Editor: Maxine Bringenberg

Chapter 1

"If you want a job here, you're going to have to cover up those tats. And by covering them, I mean I don't want to see them. At all." Ama tried her best to bring her temper down to a low simmer, but this guy was getting on her last nerve. "You think you can get rid of them by Monday?"

"No. And for the record, I wouldn't even if I could." She stood up and was moving toward the door when he called her back. She turned to look at him, not bothering to hide her contempt for the prick.

"You should have thought of this before you found yourself all drunked up and under a needle. Maybe next time you'll simply learn to say no." Opening the door, she walked out, but apparently he had more to say, so he followed her. "Maybe if you'd dress a little more conservatively, somebody might think of you less as a hooker and more of a serious worker."

She looked down at the shirt and pair of clean jeans she had on. The only thing showing besides her face and hands was her neck, and not much of it either. She had even covered the biggest mark she had on her arm by wearing long sleeves.

She looked up when he came around the doorway of the room where he'd been interviewing her and grabbed her by the arm. Ama wasn't really sure what to do now, so she did what she always did. Her fist popped out and hit him in the face before she could think to maybe take a deep breath. When he stumbled back she took a step toward him, but stopped when she realized that there were other people in the store that might step up to help the prick. She turned and walked out of the used clothing store and into the street, hiking her laptop bag up on her shoulder to keep it safe. She looked across the street and crossed against the light, then went into the deli hoping for a sandwich and a way for herself to unwind.

She was standing in line when the guy from the interview came out of his store and looked around. She turned her back, not caring at all if he saw her.

"Is that a computer?" She looked at the older woman standing next to her and nodded. "My mate and I just got ours today. I'm betting you're very good with them, aren't you?"

"I do okay. It's sort of a way of life now days." She had no idea why she was talking to her, but Ama glanced at the man coming across the street and turned back to the counter.

This time the man standing next to her spoke. "That shop you just left? The man is on his way over here. I think you should maybe try moving to one of the tables. That way if he walks by the door, he won't see you right away and maybe you might not go to jail." He laughed when she shrugged. "But if your plan is to go to jail, then by all means stand where you are and let him try and take you again. He doesn't look any too happy with you right now. When we saw you come out just in front of him, we knew he was trouble."

"Thank you, but I…he'll either leave on his own or not. I don't really care." And she didn't either. She turned her back to the man and woman again and heard the woman laugh slightly. When the door opened behind her, she didn't even bother to look. She knew who it was.

"You, Amazing or whatever the fuck your name is, I've called the police."

Ama was next in line and started to place her order. But before she could finish, she was jerked around by the asshole again. He had a white shirt held to his face, and she could see that he was still bleeding. Several people in the deli stepped back, but not the older woman or the man standing next to her.

"Good. I hope you did call them. Maybe then I can press charges against you for sexual assault." He sputtered, but she was on a roll now. "You called me a hooker and told me that I was a drunk. You're just lucky that I didn't kick your tiny little balls up around your head. I would have said brain, but it's doubtful that you have one."

He drew back to more than likely hit her, but she grabbed his balls and twisted them. He screamed like a girl.

"Now we're going to play a little game here. I'm going to call it truth or balls. The rules are simple; you tell me the truth and I won't pull your balls off. Got it?" When he didn't answer her, she gave them a little twist.

"I got it. Christ, I got it." He started to grab her arm and she twisted them again. "You're fucking going to pay for this, bitch. You see if you don't."

"Not very smart, are you? When someone has your nuts in a grip like I do, you don't threaten them. Now, did you call the police?"

He screamed when she jerked him. "No, you fucking cunt. I didn't, but you can bet your sweet ass I'm going to when I get back to my desk."

"It's doubtful that you'll be able to sit at that sorry excuse for a desk, but you're welcome to it. In a clear voice, I want

7

you to tell these nice people that you're very sorry for coming in here and ruining their lunch by cussing like a…what is it you called me again?" Ama started to twist him again until he repeated what he'd said to her in the interview, and a couple of things that he hadn't. "Good boy. Now do it."

He nearly sang out his apology and she let him go. But no sooner than she released him, he slapped her in the face. She stood there with blood running down her lip, staring him down. He was backing out of the place as he threatened her again.

Once he was out, she turned back to the man behind the counter and apologized. Then she turned to the room.

"I'm very sorry, ladies and gentlemen. I'm sorry you had to witness that." She moved to the door and was out before anyone tried to grab her. Ama was nearly a block away when a car pulled up beside her and the door was opened by the driver. The older lady from the deli and the man about her age were sitting in the back.

"We followed you." She nodded, not sure what to say. If they were pissed about the thing in the deli, they'd have to get over it. "Are we to understand that you need a job?"

All sorts of things ran through her head, none of them very clean. She wasn't into stupid shit, and she was most certainly not into anything that either of them might want with her in the back of their car. She shook her head at them and backed away.

"I'm not going to do anything perverted with you two. I may be a little on the fucked up side, but I'm not into kinky shit like that." They looked at each other, then back at her. "You have no idea what I'm talking about, do you?"

"I don't think so." The man grinned at her. "I'm assuming you mean something sexual. And if so, then you couldn't be further from the truth. We have our own kind of kinky."

The woman slapped him on the shoulder, and Ama laughed. She decided that for some odd reason she liked them. She leaned against the door and looked at the nice ride. She figured them for a lot of money, and they weren't used to it.

"What sort of job did you have in mind? I don't kill people. Well, I've not killed anyone today, though it has been tempting, and I won't wash windows. The ammonia makes me sneeze."

"No, we get the windows washed by the new help we have." The man nodded at the seat across from them. "Would you like to come inside and have a seat?"

"No thanks. You seem like a nice couple, but I read the paper all the time. People can be very distrusting, and I have to admit I'm a little more distrusting than your average person." He nodded and glanced at the woman. "You have a job that you think I can do?"

"Oh, yes, we think we do. What do you know about computers?" She nodded but didn't get a chance to answer them. "We've got one, you see. Well, laptoppers or whatever they're called, and we want to learn how to use it. Our sons Sebastian and Reed are very good with them, but they have no time to let us play around and teach us on our level."

"And your level would be what? Beginner?" They both nodded. "They're laptops, not toppers. And I'm assuming that you think they'll make fun of you if you ask them for help because of your status as their parents?"

"No. I don't think...they'd better not make fun of us. I would have to take them to the wood shed if they did. But they are quite large and sometimes a little on the vicious side when need be. We're actually thinking that Monica and Caitlynne...oh, and probably Jack and Jonny...might be a tad bit more than their mates, but we're not going to talk about them right now. Would you mind getting in? This is hard on my neck."

She looked at the driver, who stood very still. She wasn't afraid of him because she was positive she could take him if need be. She looked back at the couple in the car. The only way she was going to do this, get into a vehicle with two unknown people, was to be up front. She pulled out her gun from under her shirt and let them see it. The driver started toward her then suddenly stopped.

"I'm not going to get in there with you without you knowing that I won't be fucked with. Understand that?" They both nodded and she looked at the driver before looking back at them. "And him? Will he have a problem with this?"

"Not so long as he wants to have his throat where it is." The man had sounded so serious that she felt a slight hesitation in her step as she started toward the back with them. "You don't have to worry about us. We won't hurt you. Not so long as you don't try to hurt us first. Will you have a problem with that?"

Ama wasn't afraid of them. On the contrary, she respected them for their bullishness, but that didn't mean that she'd trust them right away. She shook her head as she sat down and left her gun on her lap. She looked at both of them as the door closed and the car started to move.

"I'm Amarizi Auburn, but most people call me Ama. Where are we going?" She watched them closely and thought they were talking to each other on their own personal wave length, which she knew their kind had. When they looked back at her, she smiled at them.

"Right now we're living with our son. He's a lovely young man, but he's a bit on the overwhelmed side right now. I believe it has to do with his new mate. We've been trying to help him, but children will be children."

She nodded, not having a clue what they were talking about. She looked out the window, then back at them. The man handed her a laptop and told her he'd just charged it up. She glanced up at them when she realized that this was no simple computer, but one that had been modified a great deal.

She handed it back to him. "I'm not stupid. I'd like very much if you'd have this guy pull over and you let me out. I don't know who you people are, but this is not even close to being a simple laptop, and it's not cheap."

"Oh my, George, we've neglected to tell her our names. I'm Corrine and this is George Bowen. And I assure you, we have no idea what you mean. Our son gave us these this morning." Corrine nodded to the other box. "He said that he'd made them easy for us to use."

Ama glared at her. "So you thought that you'd find some random person off the street to show you how to use it? I'm not buying it. You think you can entrap me, you can think again. I have no desire to go back to jail, and I'm pretty sure that even without any money, no one would believe me if I told them what really happened here."

She flushed when she realized what she'd said. She pounded on the window between the back and the driver, and when it opened, she asked him to please pull over. George told him it was okay. She was reaching for the door handle when George put his hand on her. She felt the vibration immediately and, apparently, so did he.

"Oh my." She opened the door and stepped out before he could say more. Before she was five feet from the car, he called her name.

"Amarizi, stop please." She did but didn't turn. "You know that you can't be harmed by us, and that you are a great deal stronger than either of us if you needed to be. Come back to the car and I promise you that we'll take you to our son and he can explain. We didn't know what...we had no idea when we saw you in the deli what you were, but it explains why we want to trust you. Will you please come back and let us explain?"

She turned to him slowly and saw that Corrine was standing beside him; the driver was still in the car. She looked around, noting that they were no longer in the city but on the outskirts of town in a part of town she'd never been. She looked back at him.

"I don't know what you think you know about me, but it's wrong." He nodded, all three of them knowing she was lying. "I'm going with you, but if it even looks like this son of yours doesn't have a clue what you're talking about, I'm leaving you."

He nodded, and so did Corrine, and then he opened the door for her to get in. When the car was moving again, he handed her the computer. He also handed her the box.

"My son, Sebastian Bowen, owns this store. We were just in there not an hour ago and were having lunch when that horrid man came in." Corrine smiled at her as she continued. "I thought for sure he was going to wet himself when you grabbed his more private parts."

"He called me a hooker because of my tats." Corrine nodded. "I can't help where they are." She nodded again.

"Well, of course, you can't. And he was a silly man to have thought they were tattoos and not a sigil like they actually are." She looked at her sharply. "We're not human, dear, in the event you didn't catch that. I think you might know what we are."

"Yes. Panther." She looked at the computer. "I'll help you, but you have to keep my secret to yourself. I won't have people thinking...I won't have it again."

"No, of course not. You can trust us." Ama nodded, not really sure why but she thought maybe she could. "My son will clear things right up."

~~~

George watched the young woman talk to the sales clerk. He glanced at Corrine and started to ask her what the hell they were doing. She shook her head before he could ask. When Ama stood up and walked to them, he could see that she was a lot more relaxed than she'd been before.

"It checks out. She said your son was called away on business to help one of your other sons, but what you said checks out." She looked around the store and George wondered if he could buy her anything, and wondered where that thought had come from. She looked back at him as if she knew what he'd been thinking.

"I don't want you to freak out. Are you going to?" He shook his head at her. "You look like it. If this is going to be too much for you, we can call it quits now. No sweat off me. I don't need any problems, not from you or anyone else. Especially not from any of your family, because I'm going to help you. What I'm doing is because you asked, not because of anything that might be rolling around in your head."

"My head is rolling all right. No, no, it's not that." He looked at Corrine again before turning back to her. "It's just that we thought...you must be the last of your kind."

He saw her stiffen and regretted his words, but before he could tell her how sorry he was, she spoke first. George reached for his mate, not sure why, but he needed her contact when Ama looked at him with her dark green eyes.

"You know nothing of my kind. No one does, and I'd very much like to keep it that way." He nodded and knew that the sharpness in her voice was his fault. "Do you still need me to show you this computer?"

"Yes. I would...we would very much like for you to show us how to run this." He looked at her and then opened his mouth to tell her again how profoundly sorry he was.

"Look, Mr. Bowen, we're not going to get through this if you don't just say you're sorry once and we move on. I get it, you didn't mean it. And I'm sorry, too. I shouldn't have been so short with you. But I'm a little on edge. I'm unemployed and have no place to live if I don't find something soon...I'm not asking for a hand out here, but a real job with a real paycheck would be flipping fantastic. Understand?"

"Yes, yes I do. And please call me George. And Corrine, this is Corrine." His mate nodded. "I would like to learn how to do a search on things. That's primarily what we wanted it for. Sebastian said we could do our household budget on it as well."

She nodded. "You can do just about anything on this. He's got it rigged up so that if you wanted to, you could pretty much make a movie, write books and send them out, or even download and watch movies if you wanted. He's got you set up really nicely."

"He's a good boy. All our sons are." They walked back out to the car and got in. She played around with the computer for the better part of the hour-long drive back to Khan's house, where they were staying this week while their house was being built.

"You said you wanted to learn to do some searches. You mean like on Google and stuff?"

George told her that they did. "We also want an email account. We're very new to this. I mean, we've only just gotten cell phones in the last few months and learned how to take pictures."

George looked at Corrine when she laughed. "We're not very good at sending pictures on it as yet, but we do have lots of them. We have grandchildren, you see, and we get to sit for them all the time." Ama nodded and smiled. "Then there is that site that we heard about on the television. Where you can pay all your bills at one time and not have to worry about them getting there on time."

"You might want to stay clear of them. Those sites are set up just for people like you. They'll pay out for you and right into their own account." She was putting the computer back in the box as she continued. "Most of the sites that you might want to pay online have their own payment programs. I'll show you how to set them up, but you'll enter the information if you want to use them. I won't mess with your credit cards or bank accounts other than to show you how to set them up."

George nodded. This was much more than he'd hoped for and told her so. "We thought you'd just show us how to turn it on and then find us Google. We're ever so grateful for this."

"I'm sure your son will be thrilled to death to know you picked a perfect stranger to help you. I know I would be." She grinned at him. "You're not going to tell anyone, are you? I mean what you think you know about me. What you know about me. I'm not sure how your touch over all the other times I've been randomly touched has…you can't tell anyone about me."

"No, of course we won't. We told you we wouldn't and we won't. Not even if we are asked directly by the boys." He looked over at Corrine as he continued. "We'll just say we hooked up at the deli and you agreed to help us. Not a lie. We did see you there."

George listened to his mate tell Ama about their grandkids as he tried to work through what she was. A faerie. Even as a younger man, he'd heard about them but had never thought to see one, much less meet one. Then as he got older, he'd heard that they'd been all killed. Humans hadn't understood what they were and had murdered them before they had changed into what this woman was. Nothing in the world was as strong as they were, and now there was one right in front of him that was going to show them how to use a computer.

She was lovely. Her hair was nearly white it was so blonde, and her eyes the greenest he'd ever seen. Her skin was nearly flawless, if you thought of her sigil as a flaw. But he didn't. And now that he'd touched her and had been acknowledged by her, George and his mate could see her completely. Humans would never be able to see her the way that he was right now.

The marks that were covering her eyes weren't there before. Now they could see the mask that was formed over them that looked like something one would get at Mardi Gras. The way it caught the light and sparkled made him think that she wasn't just a faerie but something more. He wondered how much more of her was marked when the limo they were riding in came to a smooth stop. She stopped him before they got out.

"You know that no one but you two can see me, right? I mean, they will see me but not the way you two do. Until I make it known to them, all they see is what everyone else can see, a woman who likes to be tattooed." George and Corrine both nodded. "If you tell anyone, do you understand what will happen?"

"We die."

Chapter 2

"Oh, and your mom and dad were in, too." Sebastian looked up from the mountain of notes that Debby, his assistant manager, had given him when he returned. "They had me talk to some woman. I think she said her name was Amazing or something like that. She said that she was giving them lessons. I thought you said they were coming here for them."

"I thought so, too." He reached for the phone to call them as Debby left the office. He'd been gone for less than three hours and had nearly fifty phone messages, and he'd not even checked his email yet. He shook his head, glad for the business, but he was beginning to feel like he needed a vacation—and soon. When someone answered his dad's cell phone, he asked what she'd said again.

"I said George Bowen's phone. Is that who you called?" He was taken aback by her answering it first of all, and by her biting tone. "Are you there?"

"Yes. Where are my parents? I want you to put them on the phone right fucking now." She snorted. "What have you done to them?"

"I've thrown them in the basement and am right now ransacking their house. And I was just calling for a cab to

17

come and get me out here in the fucking wilderness when you called. And for a lark, I thought I'd answer and incriminate myself." He was so startled that he didn't know what to say. "They're right here, dumbass."

"Hello, dear. Your dad is trying to do a search for raspberry tea, and then it's my turn. I have to think of something to look up. Do you have any ideas for me?" He said the first thing that popped into his head. "Oh no, Sebastian, I have to look up something I don't know anything about. I know a great deal about herbs."

"Then look up how to put together a jet engine." He took a deep breath. "Who is that who answered the phone, and why is she answering Dad's phone in the first place?"

"Her name is Ama. Well that's not her real name. Her real name is Amarizi. Amarizi Auburn. She's been ever so helpful to us. She helped us set up our accounts on line and we have an email account, too." She sounded so excited that he nearly smiled. But the woman was probably robbing them blind.

"I just bet you are. I was wondering if I may have a few words with her. Just to make sure that she isn't steering you in the wrong direction." He tried to smile to make his voice sound less like he was grinding nails with his teeth. She told him to wait until her turn and then she'd put her on.

Sebastian could hear her speaking but not exactly what she was saying. There was something muffled about her voice and he wasn't happy with that. For all he knew she could be setting them up with accounts that led directly to her account, and his parents would be dead by the time he got there. Standing up, he was headed out of the office and to his car when she came on the line. He didn't wait for her to say any more than hello before he tore into her.

"You hurt my mother and father and you will never be able to hide deep enough. And if they don't have every single penny in their account that they had before, I—"

"Listen to me, you paranoid mother fucking prick. If I wanted them dead, they'd have been so in the back of the limo that we came here in. If I wanted their money, do you think that you threatening me is going to make me give it back? Fuck off." He heard his dad say something. "Your father wants to talk to you, but I have just one more thing to say. If you ever—and I mean ever—threaten me or accuse me of something you have absolutely no knowledge of again, I will tear you apart."

Sebastian stumbled to his car. Terror, not for his parents but for himself, rolled over him. He felt her threat to him as if she'd been standing right in front of him and had delivered it to him face to face. He felt his panther roll away as if she'd been bigger, meaner than him, and now he was curling away from her. His dad saying his name made him think that he'd said it more than once.

"Sebastian? I think I might have lost him." He could hear the anger in his dad's voice and that of his mom. But the woman said nothing.

"I'm here, Dad. What is she doing there? And did she mean that she'd been in—?"

"You had no right. None at all to upset her like that. I swear to you if you were here right now, I'd beat you within an inch of your life. She's been helping us all day. All damned day and we were having so much...I wish you were here. I wish that you were right here so I could paddle your behind. You had no right to talk to our friend like you did."

"Dad, I'm sorry, but what do you know about this person? For all you know, she could be—" He realized he was talking to dead air. "Mother fuck."

He actually had his arm back to throw his phone, but it rang again. He hoped it was his dad calling back, but the tone told him it was his brother Marc. He answered, wondering if he'd already heard how pissed he'd made Dad.

"I was wondering if you could come by and help me with something. I got a new television today and I'm having trouble hooking up the cable lines. I don't have the colored wires that they said—"

"Did you read the fucking instructions?" He closed his eyes as soon as the words left his mouth. "I'm sorry."

"No shit. Would you like to start over, or would you like for me to come down there and kick your ass for speaking to me that way? Might make you feel better in the long run. I know it would me." Marc laughed. "Wanna come by and have a beer with me and Jonny? Well, I'm having a beer, and she's having a glass of tea. And pizza?"

"Maybe. But first I have to go and tell Dad that I'm sorry, and then apologize to some woman they have helping them play on the Internet." He got into his car and started it up. "I'm pretty sure that I'm going to be on the shit list for a very long time."

"That doesn't sound like you. What did you say to her?" Sebastian told him. "Christ, buddy, you'll be lucky if you ever get off it with that. I can see why Dad is mad. Hang on."

He was put on hold and decided to put in his earphone and talk and drive. Sebastian didn't text while driving and he never looked at his phone either. There was a time and place for that, and going sixty miles an hour down a highway wasn't the time or the place. His brother was laughing when he came back on.

"I wouldn't go to Dad right now if I was you. He's spitting mad and said he's going to get a switch. Man, I don't think I've ever heard him cuss like that." Sebastian groaned.

"If I were you, I'd give him until tomorrow, and then maybe you might live to tell about it."

"I think I'll just get it over with. They're all there now and I can just go and take my medicine like a man. I'm pretty sure that whatever he has planned for me is nothing I've not thought of doing to myself. I was way out of line."

He pulled into Khan's drive and got out a few minutes after hanging up with Marc, who had told him to come by after he received his punishment. Sebastian told him that he'd think about it. His parents' car wasn't in the drive and his mom came out just as he was ready to step on the lowest step.

"I hope you're very proud of yourself." He hung his head in shame. "Look at me when I'm talking to you, young man."

His head snapped up like she'd jerked it up. "I'm sorry, Mom. I was having a bad day and I took it out on her. I have no excuse for what I did."

"No, you do not." She didn't move and he stayed where he was. "You embarrassed us. And her. Do you know that we'd tried to pay her all afternoon and she wouldn't take a penny from us? Then you call and first off accuse her of theft and all sorts of other things."

"She told you what I said?" He dropped his head again when she glared at him. He heard the door open and knew it was his dad. Sebastian could feel his anger as if he was throwing it at him.

"She didn't say anything other than that she had to leave. Was going to walk back to the city, but I had to make her ride in with that man you guys have driving us all over. Wouldn't let me go with her to make sure she got home all right, saying you'd be mad. Well, damn it, boy, I'm mad!" His dad's voice thundered down at him. "What did you say to her? We heard her all right, but not a thing you were saying."

21

"I accused her of stealing your money when she set up the accounts, and that she was planning to murder you after she got all your money." He looked up at them both. "What the hell was I supposed to think when I hear my own parents have gone to someone else for help with a computer and not their own son?"

"You'd think that we were capable of making sound decisions on our own." That hurt him coming from his mom. "She set up the email account and all the other accounts, but never once put in a single thing that we would call ours. Our passwords...she stepped away when we put them in, as well as the credit card numbers to the accounts that we have that pay our electric and phone bills. She even cautioned us about using one of those sites that can pay them for you, and told us to never save our passwords on the computer but to write them down in a notebook."

All the things he would have done for him. He looked up at his dad. He had really hurt him and he knew it. He started up the steps when the limo pulled back into the driveway. His dad walked to the driver without a word to him, and Sebastian knew that his dad would be hard pressed to forgive him.

"Mom, I never meant to make you think that you couldn't do all this on our own. I would have helped you." She shook her head. "I would have."

"Maybe, but lately you've been...well, short with everyone, and we wanted to surprise you with what we could do. We, your father and I, had so much fun until you called. She was laughing with us and joking with your dad's choice of sites he wanted to look into. She even told us that she'd had fun."

"Until I called." She nodded. "I'm going to apologize to her. Just tell me when she'll be back and I'll be here to tell her how sorry I am."

"I don't think she's coming back." He heard the hurt in her voice. "I doubt we'll see her again. I'm pretty sure that she...I don't think she'll come back."

When she turned her back to him and entered the house, Sebastian sat on the steps. Pain shot through him as if he'd been stabbed right in his heart. When his dad came toward him, Sebastian thought for sure he was going to go around him without speaking, but he stopped.

"You embarrassed us. And you hurt your mom. We were having a grand time with her and you messed it up because you don't trust us." He couldn't even deny that. "You should go home. I'll see you tomorrow."

"Dad, I'm so sorry." His dad nodded and went into the house.

Sebastian started for his car but bypassed it for the limo driver. He walked up to him and asked him where he'd taken the girl.

"She's got herself a place at the Y, Mr. Bowen. I didn't know if I got her back in time for her to be able to get in, but that lady that runs the place said she'd let her in." Sebastian asked him what she'd looked like. "Looks like? I tried to think on that when I dropped her off. I remember thinking that she was pretty, but right now I couldn't tell you a thing about her. Don't you think that's a little strange?"

Strange maybe for someone else's family, but not his. He nodded to the driver and walked to his car. He called Marc and told him he was going home, that he was never going to be able to dig himself out of this one.

"Find your mate and knock her up. I'm telling you, it's like having a get-out-of-jail-free card. You can't do anything wrong."

Sebastian told him he'd work on that and drove home. It was going to be a long night.

~~~

Ama stripped down and lay on the bed. She was looking up at the light when she thought of the man on the phone. Man, he had one suspicious nature about him. She rolled to her side and smiled at the fun she'd had with the elder Bowens. They had made her laugh all afternoon. And they'd made sure that she was welcome, something she'd not felt in anyone's home before.

The phone ringing outside her room had her listening to see if anyone would answer it. Lately it had been for someone named Carol. Ama was pretty sure that Carol had left about two weeks ago owing a great deal of money to the people who ran this place. When it rang five times, it finally stopped. She never answered it, as no one but the Bowen's driver knew where she was.

Getting up to get the paper, she wrapped a sheet around her nudity. She didn't mind being naked, especially when the air was cool like it was now. She felt her sigil hum along her skin but for the most part ignored it. She had to find a job.

Her last job had been great. She'd worked as a telemarketer for a large cell phone firm. No one had to see her and she could wear pretty much anything she'd wanted, but when the building burned down about four months ago, they'd decided to go to another location to set up business and it was too far for her to walk. She didn't know how to drive, and couldn't afford a car anyway. But she'd gotten unemployment and a nice fat bonus check, and that money was still hidden in one of her shoes. She wasn't going to touch that unless it was an emergency, because she was going to buy a house and grow plants in the backyard.

She still had plenty of unemployment left, about a year if she needed it, but she didn't like not working. She was starting to feel listless and out of sorts and knew it was because she wasn't working. Then there was the lack of sleep.

Ama could sleep for only four hours a day, if that. And she needed to eat, a lot. Her species, she supposed, had a great deal to do with that in that she burned a great deal more energy than humans.

She thought of the Bowens and them knowing what she was. Last of her kind? She thought she was but had no way of really knowing. She thought her mom was dead but wasn't sure. And since she had no clue who her dad was, she just assumed he was dead, too. She wasn't really sure what she'd been until about five years ago when someone had touched her, like the Bowens had, and called her an earth faerie.

The man had been very nice. He'd told her that he'd seen others like her, but none of them had been a purebred as she was. He explained to her in great detail what was going to happen to her when she turned twenty-five and why, and he'd been dead on the money. After spending about a week with her, he'd simply disappeared, warning her that she must tell all those that figured out what she was that if they told anyone else they would die. He told her that most beings, if they'd ever heard of her, would know that anyway. She wondered what had ever happened to him.

Her thoughts turned to the man, Sebastian, again. She'd tried her best not to think of the things he'd said to her, but it was hard. She really didn't blame him for wanting to protect his parents; she might have done the same thing. But he'd caught her off guard being so mean to her after she'd had such a wonderful time with his parents. She supposed that by now George and Corrine had forgiven him and he was no longer going to get his hide stripped off him like they'd threatened. She smiled as she got back into the bed, realizing that she'd not seen anything in the paper because she wasn't really reading it.

The phone started ringing again. She knew that at midnight someone from the offices would come around and take it off the hook so that it didn't bother anyone. She also knew that it was so that the woman at the desk could read her books without interruptions. Ama thought the woman read to escape whatever drama was going on at home, because sometimes she'd hear her arguing with someone on the phone. She didn't know if she had children, but the person on the phone seemed to take great pleasure in making her cry nightly.

Finding a job was proving to be the biggest hurdle she'd had in a while. Before she'd worked for the telemarketer she'd been a waitress, but since her face had decided to betray her, she'd had to find work that put her behind the scenes rather than in front of the customers. Even working in a pizza shop had been hard with having to go to the counter sometimes. People would stare at her and she'd be pissed. The manager finally told her one night, after there was a line of teenagers in to ask her about themselves, that she was more of a hindrance than a help to him. She left with her last check and an extra-large all the way that she'd given to some homeless man under the bridge.

She decided she was going to find a job tomorrow even if she had to put a bag over her head to do it.

The phone ringing woke her up. She looked at the clock above her bed and rolled out of it. Whoever it was wanted the girl named Carol really bad. It was barely six in the morning and it was already starting. Gathering her things, she went to the shower just outside her room. Might as well get a start.

She was back only about ten minutes when a girl, someone she'd never seen before, knocked on her open door. Ama looked at her, trying to remember if she actually knew her or not. The girl cleared that up in a hurry.

"Are you, Ama? If you are, this guy's been calling here. Says his name is Sebastian something. He wants you to call him back as soon as it's convenient for you." Ama started to tell her she didn't know anyone by that name, but the girl spoke first. "He sounds kinda yummy. And nice, too. I'll call him if you want me to."

She remembered then...Sebastian Bowen. "If he calls again, tell him that I'm not upset and I don't want to talk to him. Tell him to stop bothering you."

"Sure, but he's not bothering me. So you don't want him? I can have him?"

Ama nodded and turned back to the newspaper's wanted ads. As the girl mumbled her thanks Ama stood up.

She was hitting the first place by a little after seven. The guy took one look at her and simply shook his head. She was well on her way to the third place when she saw the Bowens again. Ducking down an alley, she waited until she was sure they were gone before she stepped out again. More problems like the ones she had with their son she didn't need.

By lunchtime she'd hit five places and had only filled out one application. She went into the restaurant of the Greek place down from the comic shop and ordered, and then went to the bathroom. The mirror over the sink seemed to mock her.

Her eyes were a very pretty shade of green, and that was about all her looks said in a positive way. Closing her eyes, she willed her face to look like the humans saw it. When she opened them and looked, she was surprised again, like she was every time she saw the differences.

Right between her brows was a diamond-shaped, emerald-looking mark. And from it there were intricate twists and curves that formed a line just above her eyebrows that were a darker green than the emerald. These lines extended down past her eyes and into her hairline, where they curved around her ears and then to the back of her neck to her back. A few smaller twists were on her throat, but weren't as easy to see.

Her hands were clear of any marks as humans saw her. But when she looked at herself, her complete self, she could see herself as she truly was. The same dark green lines were there, but with more diamond shapes in all the colors of the world. She doubted that if anyone saw these they'd ever believe they were done by a needle. They were too detailed, too brightly colored, and most assuredly not drawn by a human hand. Before she could think about her back, she heard someone coming toward the bathroom and closed her eyes again. The problem with looking at herself as they saw her was that they could see the real her. She was just splashing water on her face when the woman and a small child came in behind her.

The child was perhaps three or four, but she stared at Ama like she could see her as she really was; which, according to Jacob, she more than likely could. Winking at her, Ama left them to their business and went to order her lunch. A large chicken gyro and fries later, she was headed back to a much shorter list than she'd hoped. As she walked into the last place on her list, she nearly turned around and left.

The man at the counter was big. She never took her eyes off him as she moved toward him. This could go really badly for them both, because she was pretty sure he knew just what she was.

"Mistress." He bowed his head at her. "What is it I can help you with? I am at your service."

She looked at the door. She could just leave and he would simply have a story to tell. But she wanted a job, and he needed someone to wash dishes. Ama walked up to the counter and nodded to him.

"I'm Amarizi Auburn. I need a job." He nodded. "You have an ad in the paper that says you need a dishwasher. Have you filled it?"

He shook his head and smiled. "You're an earth faerie. It would be an honor to have you working the floor, mistress. The dishwasher job is for someone well beneath you."

"No, it's not. I'm just Ama the dishwasher and nothing more. Got it?" He stared at her for several seconds, then threw back his head and laughed. She turned to the door to leave, nearly to the point of tears. He stopped her by calling her name.

"I'm sorry, but we both know that you're much more than Ama the dishwasher." She shook her head, and he stared at her for a full minute before nodding. "All right. I need a dishwasher, and for your own reasons you need to work. Can you start tonight?" She nodded. "Come back around five and work until around two in the morning? The weekends are the busiest. I'll need you later then."

She nodded, so grateful that she wanted to hug him, but only nodded again. He didn't touch her when she was handed the application, and she was happy for that. He said his name was Peter Gunn, and Peter was a black bear.

Chapter 3

Sebastian was looking at the broken laptop when his assistant came in. Debby sat down across from him and sighed heavily. There was no way he was going to ask her what was wrong again. He'd done that before and had been sucked into so much drama that he'd wanted to fire her. He looked up at her and asked her how sales were going.

"Great. The new stuff is out on the shelves. I'm thinking of using my discount and getting the new unit you brought in for the readers. Man, that sucker can do it all." He nodded and put the cover back on the dead laptop. He'd known it was a bust when it was brought to him, but said he'd give it a shot.

"I'm not going to be here after four. My family is having a big dinner tonight and I want to be there on time." He didn't add that he was trying to score some major brownie points with his parents or that he'd been threatened by his brothers and sisters-in-law to be nice. "Will you have a problem closing up?"

"No. I guess not." He tried his best to look like he didn't care. "Mark and I broke up today. He said that I was just too much for him."

Sebastian didn't ask. He stood up to put the laptop on the shelf to give back to the man who'd brought it in. Who would do this to a computer that they'd paid over nine hundred dollars for was beyond him. The man had admitted to "accidently" dropping it out his car window. Really? Not likely. He realized that Debby was waiting on him to say something. He had no idea what she'd been saying to him.

"I don't know, Debby. What do you think?" He'd used this before on his dates when he'd tuned them out over dinner. It worked well for him so long as he tried to remember if he'd used it once already. They got sort of pissy when you repeated it several times over the salad.

"I just want him to marry me. What makes men want to run in the other direction when a woman starts talking about weddings and children?" With her, Sebastian could think of a list a mile long, but kept his mouth shut as she continued. "I mean, it's not like we just met, for crap's sake. We've been dating for almost a whole month."

A month? He suddenly felt sorry for the guy. Debby could do a good job when she was focused, but there were times when he thought she would be better off working at a job where she had little contact with the outside world and simply lived in her own little world she had created. One that made her the queen of the universe and where no one told her no. She was scary weird. But she was good at selling, and that alone gave her job security.

The bell over the door sounded and she hopped up and ran out to the floor. He was sure that the other employee could have handled it. All his employees were very knowledgeable about the products they sold, but Debby had to be right there. Sebastian decided that he was going to have to make some serious changes soon.

"It's your dad. He wants to know if he can come back and talk to you." He looked at James, the other employee, and nodded. "Oh, and your mom is here, too, but she wants to just look around."

Sebastian was nearly around his work station when his dad came in the room. Before he could ask him if everything was all right, he was pulled into a hug that nearly took his breath away. Sebastian hugged his dad just as hard and felt the tears threaten. He'd missed his dad.

"I'm sorry, son." He patted him on the back before turning away. "I shouldn't have…damn, I was a fool, just like your mom says to me daily."

"No, Dad, I was." It had been almost a week since the conversation about the girl and the computer. "I should have given you more time with the computer, and I shouldn't have said those things to either of you. You've no idea how horrible I've felt."

"Me too, me too. It's been like a hole in my heart. I'm glad…." He took a deep breath. "I was wondering if you found Ama. She said that day that she wouldn't be able to help us any, said that she wasn't gonna come between a man and his son. She said a great deal more, but I won't repeat it. Not that at the time I didn't think you deserved it, but there you have it."

Sebastian laughed. He was pretty sure she had said a great deal. And his dad was right, he had deserved it. That and more. He'd blown up at her and she'd only fought back. His mom walked in as they were both sitting down.

"I was just asking Sebastian here if he'd heard from Ama. I think he was about to tell us he's right on top of it." His dad looked at him. "Are you?"

"I tried to reach out to her, but she told the operator that she was fine and that I wasn't to bother her anymore." He flushed when he thought of what else the operator had told him and had asked him, but decided that there was no way he was telling them that conversation. "She's living at the 'Y.'"

He was thinking about Sandy the operator and some of the things she'd suggested he could do with her and to her when he realized that his parents were looking at each other oddly. There was something going on and he sat up in his chair and waited for them to get finished with whatever it was they were talking about. When his mom turned to him, she looked nervous.

"We need for you to find her for us, to tell her it's okay that she helped us learn the computer like she did." He started to tell her that he was going to do it when she spoke again. "There's something about her that we found…she's not like us, but she's more than us. I can't tell you any more than that, but she…I think she needs us."

He looked at his dad, hoping for more to go on, but he was nodding. "I told you I tried to talk to her and she told the woman who answers the phone that I wasn't to contact her any more. She told me that there would be police involved if I did."

Sebastian had been and still was a little upset about that part, but he had been very threatening to her. He thought involving the police was a little much, but could see now if what his parents were telling him was true then maybe he'd frightened her more than he'd thought.

"Then we'll go to Marc. He would be able to make sure that we get to talk to her and—" Sebastian stood up and walked to his mom. "We need to find her. It's really important to us. To all of us."

"What is she?" His mom looked at his dad, then back at him. Something was off here. When he started to ask her again, she shook her head.

"We can't tell you that. Not that I wouldn't love to share this, but we can't. It's dangerous. Not for you but for us if we repeat what we've been given."

"Mom, that makes no sense. What did she make you promise? And what did she threaten you with?" He looked at his dad when she did. "Dad? What is it you're not telling me?"

"I'm sorry, son. You'll just have to trust us. She's very important to us and…well, to all of us. We want to make sure she's all right."

They left a little while later, and he sat at his desk trying to figure out what to do now. He'd told them that he'd find the girl for them. He wasn't sure why he just didn't let them go to Marc with this. He was better equipped to find people, and he was just a computer person. Picking up the phone, he decided to ask him how to start.

"You have her name?" He told him. "I can start a search for her and see…. Well what do you know? I found her. She's working for a friend of yours, Peter Gunn. He already filed her work papers and such. She's working for him at his place over on Main."

She had a job. He had no idea why that surprised him, but it did. He supposed it had to do with his parents wanting to find her, and him thinking that she owed them money or something. He supposed that she could still owe them, but she had a job, so that helped. He thanked his brother and decided to have pizza for lunch.

~~~

"You're doing a great job, mistress." She looked at Peter and didn't even bother trying to ask him again just to call her

Ama. He seemed to be sort of old fashioned, and she was kind of sweet on him anyway. He was like the dad she'd never had. She smiled at him.

"It's not hard. Scrape, rinse, and load. Then when they come out the other side, stack and put away." He laughed with her. "I like it and it's paying the bills."

She had started looking at apartments yesterday. She needed to get something that was more in line with her hours. She wasn't getting back until well after lock-up, and that was going to be a problem soon. The lady who ran the night desk was retiring soon, and Ama needed something more anyway. She also wanted something of her own.

"I've heard of a place you can stay, too. I wish you'd let me put you up. It would be an honor." She shook her head, and he nodded as he continued. "It's not much, just a room with a bath. But it's a month-to-month place, and you won't need to put down a deposit. I know the owner."

"Do you think they'll care?" She flushed, hating that she had to ask if someone was going to freak out when they first saw her. He shook his head and laughed.

"Nah, he won't care. Nice guy, and isn't human either. And since I know you, there's no reason for you to have any contact with him. I told him you were a nice kid, just needed a little help. You'll just have to pay him once a month and that'll be the end of your relationship with him."

She nodded and he was called away. She was just pulling on her coat when she heard him laugh. He had a laugh that made a person smile. She was out the door and into the street a few minutes later.

He'd given her the address, so she headed over there. She didn't have a lot of stuff, just clothes and a few things like that, but as far as furniture went, nothing at all. She was standing in front of the building when something felt as if it touched her. She looked around and didn't see anything, but looked back at the building. There was something off about it.

Ama walked closer to the large brick building, trying to decide if whatever she'd felt had been good or bad, when she heard a muffled scream. Not thinking about anything but getting to where it had come from, she came upon a man holding a woman against the wall, tearing at her clothes.

"You should really let her go." The man turned to her and stilled. "I mean, she doesn't look to me like she's happy with whatever it is you think you're going to do to her. So let her go. Please."

"Get the fuck out of here before you're next." She nodded, thinking that he'd have to be really stupid if he thought she was going to wait until he finished with the woman just so she could have a turn. She took several steps to him before he pulled the woman to his chest and put a knife to her throat. Ama stopped just a few feet from him.

"You really shouldn't do this. I mean, she doesn't want this, and neither do I." He pressed the knife harder into the woman's throat, and Ama shrugged. "You should have listened."

The woman went limp just as Ama had told her to, and she closed her eyes. Reaching for the man, Ama grabbed his arm that held the knife and jerked him hard. She knew that she'd hurt him because he started screaming the moment she pulled him forward and away from the woman. A sharp pain in her arm made her wince, but she tossed the man away from her at the same moment his knife fell to the ground. As soon as he hit the wall, she knew that she'd thrown him just a little too hard. She heard the crush of his bones, and then he fell to the earth. Before she looked at him, she turned to the woman who now held the knife in her hands. This was not going to go well.

"Are you hurt?" Ama had to ask her three times before she said she was. "I'd very much like for you to put the knife down before someone gets hurt."

"He was going to rape me." Ama nodded at her softly spoken statement. "He was going to kill me, wasn't he?"

"More than likely. Can you put the knife down please?" The woman looked at it as if she hadn't realized she had it. When it dropped to the ground, Ama took a deep breath and kicked it away. "Do you have a cell phone that you can use to call the police? I think he's hurt badly."

He was but that didn't matter right now. The girl nodded, walked to where she'd been held, and picked up her purse. While she dialed the number, Ama went to the man. She had to help him if she could.

He was breathing, but just barely. Looking at the girl who was finally falling apart, screaming at the police that a man had tried to kill her, Ama turned back to the man and put her hand on him. She felt the power surge through her in seconds. The man stirred a little, then looked up at her.

"What the fuck did you do to me?" She didn't say anything but backed up. He watched her for several seconds before he closed his eyes again. Ama stood between them both and waited for the siren.

The first officer on the scene walked to them with his gun out. He had both her and the woman put their hands up.

By the time the third cruiser showed up, the man was being treated. Mary Scott, the woman, was also having her wounds looked at. Apparently, she'd been coming home from work downtown when he'd grabbed her before going into her apartment. She lived in the building that Ama was going to be living in, too.

"Did he tell you anything?" Mary shook her head, then nodded. "Which is it? Did he tell you something or not?"

Like her, the woman was marked, only Mary's was a tattoo. She had a dragon on her throat that was small, but colorful, and the cop had sneered at them both when he'd seen it. She was ready to pop him in the mouth when another man, another panther, came forward.

"Officer James, I think you can bring it down a notch or two. These women have been through an ordeal and you're not helping them." Another man made his way to them as the second one spoke. She watched as he took a small stumble when he saw her. Then he stopped moving.

"Look at them, Captain. How do we know they didn't work this out before we got in and roll the man for his wallet? I mean, just look at them. They look like they've been at this game for a long while." The first man, James, pointed at her. "And that one, she claims she was just passing by. Women like her deserve what they get."

Her fist was out and headed toward his face when she was suddenly stopped by a shout of "No." The man who'd stumbled was standing between her and the cop, and Ama took a step back from him. He was flipping huge.

"He's not worth it."

She nodded slowly, not sure what was going on when the second cop, the captain, nodded too. "This is my brother Marc. I'm Khan. Are you…are you…Christ, what are you?"

She took another step back and then another, and looked around for a way to escape. Things were getting just a little too much for her. When Khan closed the distance by half, she held up her hand.

"Don't touch me." He nodded and looked at Marc. "I don't know what you're thinking, but I'm just a dishwasher. And I didn't attack that man. He was trying to rape her."

"I didn't think you had." He looked at her hard, then took another step forward. "You're hurt. Come back to the ambulance and let them have a look at you."

"No. I don't have any money for that. And even if I did, I'm not going anywhere. I have to be at work again soon and I'll be fine." She looked down at the blood staining her shirt where the man had cut her. "I just want to go in and see if the apartment is still for rent."

Khan looked at his brother, and she knew that they were communicating through their link. When Khan looked back at her, he was frowning. She looked around again for a way to leave. But she was in an alley, and he and his brother were blocking her way out.

"You wouldn't be Amazing…Amazing something, would you?" She shook her head. "Then what's your…my name is Khan Bowen. Do you know my parents?"

She paled and took a step back, wondering which one of these men were there to tell her to stay the fuck away from their parents, or if it was both of them. "I didn't hurt them and I didn't take their money. I don't want any problems. I've stopped helping them. That should be enough for you."

Khan laughed. "I would say that was for Sebastian. He's our other brother. Marc here works on and off for the police when they need him, but he has his own investigating firm, and I…I'm the leader of my family now that my dad has retired. They—our parents—have been worried about you. You were at my house when Sebastian called you."

"He was very rude to me." Khan nodded and braced his arms over his chest. "I've told him that there was no reason to pursue me. I said that things are fine and I've been avoiding your parents. If you're detaining me here for that reason, I can assure you that I won't—"

"I'm not detaining you, miss. I'm concerned, that's all. I'd like for you to come with me to the house and let my mom look at your wound. Then as soon as they're assured that you're going to be all right, I swear to you that I'll bring you right back here." He looked up at the apartment building. "Of course, I should warn you that Sebastian owns this building. I don't know what you'll think about staying here now that you know, but I…well, I had to warn you."

That did complicate things a little. She looked at Marc to see that he was talking with a couple of other cops. James wasn't around, and she had a moment to wonder if he was hiding out to get her. But when she looked at Khan, he smiled at her.

"He won't bother you again." She shivered. There was something very scary about his tone that made her almost feel sorry for the officer if he ever tried to speak to her again.

"I will go to your house, but I don't really need to have my wound looked at. It will heal soon." Which it would, as soon as she ate something. "If I say that I'll go with you to see to your parents, you'll bring me back here? You can't lie to me."

"Yes. You have my word." He looked at her for a few seconds. "I can't lie to you, can I? You never told me what you are."

"No, I didn't. And I don't plan on it either. If you'd be so kind as to let me finish here, I'll go with you, but I cannot stay. I do have a job and I need to work. Mr. Gunn was kind enough to give me one and I won't leave him hanging."

"Peter Gunn?" She nodded. "He's a good man. I'm guessing that you know what he is, as well as my brother and me?"

"Yes. I know what all the paranormals are here and anywhere else I go." She looked at Marc as he approached them again. "Do I need to fill out any paperwork?"

"No, you're fine. I've taken care of everything for you. I might have to come by and see you sometime soon to fill out a statement, but until then, you're free to go."

Chapter 4

Sebastian was just pulling into the driveway of Khan's house when his brother pulled in behind him. He was surprised to see Marc as well and a woman with them, but only nodded to them and asked to speak to Marc. When the other two went into the house, Sebastian looked at Marc.

"Who's that? Never mind. I have enough problems right now." Marc laughed. "I want you to do a background on that woman I was telling you about. She's apparently talked Peter into her taking one of the apartments at the building I own."

"I know." Sebastian started to ask him how he knew when Marc nodded to the house. "That's her, your tenant. She stopped a man from raping one of your other tenants today and was cut. Khan brought her back here so that Mom and Dad could see that she's fine. Of course, she's not but she said she'd heal."

Sebastian started toward the house, then stopped. He'd made a scene with her and if he went in there now, he might again. He was debating on just leaving and coming back some other time when Marc slapped him on the back as he started for the house.

"What do you think they're going to think of you if you just leave now?" He was right and Sebastian followed him to the steps. "But if I were you, I'd keep my mouth shut. She handled a man tonight without anything more than her hands. I'm pretty sure one panther isn't going to cause her one bit of a problem. Not to mention Khan says she's something powerful and makes him want to bow down before her."

He paused before stepping onto the steps. Powerful? Christ, just what they needed, something in the house that made Khan nervous. He moved into the kitchen and noticed that the only people there were the cook and Khan. He asked if their parents were there.

"Mom is taking care of Ama's cut. Monica is showing Dad what she was able to figure out for him on some search he was doing, and Bill and I were discussing the finer arts of a hamburger grilled on the grill or one in a pan. Which do you prefer?"

Sebastian sat down. His brother apparently knew all about his parents and his fight with Ama. He started to explain when the door opened and his mom walked in. Then a very beautiful woman came in behind her. Sebastian felt as if he had been hit with a two-by-four.

"Sebastian, sit down, you're making her nervous." He glanced at Khan when he whispered through his mind. *"She's ready to bolt and if she does, you're going to be in more trouble now then you were just a few days ago. Sit the fuck down."*

He sat down, but felt the need to stand when she smiled at them all. His mom nodded toward them all as she spoke. "Everyone, this is Amarizi Auburn. She's the young lady that helped your father and me when we got our computers. She's come to tell me that she's okay, and she's agreed to help us when she can next week."

"So that explains the Amazing part. I remembered something about your first name but not how to say it. I think

Ama suits better anyway." Khan offered her a seat which she took, as far from him as she could get. "Would you like to stay for dinner? We're having some sort of burgers. I just don't know if they're grilled or fried."

"I can't. I have to get back to work." She glanced at Sebastian, then back at Khan. "Can you take me now? I have to get back there before five."

Sebastian felt the low growl come up from his chest and spill from his mouth. Everyone turned to him as he stood. As soon as his mom stepped in front of Ama, he started forward.

"Don't touch me." The words were low, coming from Ama, but they only seemed to fuel him. "If you come any closer, I will hurt you."

Sebastian hadn't realized he'd been moving until he looked at his mom's face. She looked furious and her cat moved along her skin. She would attack him if he moved to Ama. Taking a deep breath confirmed what his cat and his body were already telling him. Ama was his.

"I need to touch her." His mom looked at Khan as he moved up behind Ama, and Sebastian felt the need to kill wash over him. "Khan, you have to move away from her. If you don't, I'm going to kill you."

Khan seemed to freeze in place but took a step back. "I didn't know. I had no...Monica is coming. She's not happy with you."

Monica came into the room just as Khan finished speaking. Her cat looked ready to do battle because Sebastian had threatened her mate. Sebastian put up his hands and waited for her to move around him. Her body was tense and ready for him to make a move so she could leap at his throat. He looked up in time to see Ama move toward the door.

"If you leave here, I'm going to chase you. And there's no way you're leaving here with my brother, any of them. Sit."

As soon as the words left his mouth, he knew that he'd fucked up. But the blood running through his veins was hot with both the need to take her as his mate and to hurt anyone who tried to keep him from her.

Suddenly he found himself across the room and held hard against the cabinets. No one was touching him, but he knew it was Ama who held him there. She stepped nearer to him but never let him down. Sebastian stared at her as her body took on a change that took his breath away.

Her eyes now glowed to a bright green, and her hair, white as the brightest light, was flying about her shoulders like she was in a storm. He was pretty sure they were. The tat around her eyes started to morph and change, too. Before it was just above her brows. Now it grew to cover her cheeks and forehead, which were glowing brightly as well.

"You do not talk to me that way." He nodded as she pointed her finger at his chest. "I'm a person not a…not a…."

"Dog? No, you're not. I don't know what you are, but you're not a dog." Sebastian opened his mouth to take more of her scent in. "Christ, you're beautiful and smell delicious. Let me down now, please, Amarizi. I want to take you right now. I need to mark you right fucking now."

He noticed that his family had left the room. Amarizi started to pace, and he asked her again to let him down. She didn't even look in his direction, and he stayed right where she held him.

"That man said you'd be difficult. He told me that someday a man would come to me and claim me. He said that once he did, all my…." She turned to look at him, anger burning in her eyes. "You're not going to do anything to me. I refuse to be any man's mate. I don't like what I am now, and I won't have any more of this…this thing unleashed. You'll stay away from me."

46

"I don't think you understand. I won't be able to now. I've found you and.... Do you think we could have this conversation without me dangling three feet off the ground? It's a little disconcerting to think you can do this to me."

He felt himself being lowered and when he reached for her, she slammed him hard against the cabinets again. This time only his head hit, and he stayed on the floor. He'd be glad when she couldn't hurt him. His head was beginning to ache pretty badly right now.

"I said you're not to touch me." He nodded and sat slowly in the chair. He also left his hands flat on the table, not giving her any excuse to toss him around again. When she started to pace again, he noticed that her hands were tight in her pockets. He wondered what she was hiding there.

"I would very much like to know what you are. I know that you can't be human because of the marks on your face. Those aren't tats like I first thought, but a part of you." She nodded. "You're powerful, and I would imagine that you're even now trying to hold a great deal of that in you. Are you hurting?"

"You have no idea how much I want to be naked and be what I was meant to be. I don't want to be this. I...." She pulled her hands from her pockets then and yanked her sleeve up. "This is moving along my skin like it wants to be free. Like if I were to go outside and strip down that I could change and be what I.... I want your brother to take me back where he found me, and for you to never come near me again." The marks on her arm were moving, the web-like marks almost pulsing. He desperately wanted to touch her, but she backed up when he answered her.

"That's not possible, and I think you know that as well." He stood and she backed away from him more. He let her as he moved to the cabinet and took out two glasses. "I take it my mom knows what you are, as well as my dad. Can I know?"

He poured them both a glass of iced tea and sat one across from him at the table and took his to the other end and sat down with it. He wasn't sure she would sit, and he had no idea why he knew she needed something sweet to drink, but he sat very still waiting for her to move. When she sat down and picked up the glass and drained it, he pushed his toward her. She did the same to it.

"Thank you. I need a lot of sweets when I'm stressed." She looked at him as he stood up, got the pitcher, and poured both glasses full again. She picked up the third glass and drank it down, and shook her head when he asked her if she needed a refill.

"Can we start over?" She looked at him, panicky, and he smiled. "I mean from the beginning. My name is Sebastian Bowen. My parents are Corrine and George. As you know, I'm a panther, a full blood. I own the computer store downtown where you met my assistant, Debby, the other day."

"I'm not sure she's all there. Debby, I mean. She is a woman who has some major commitment issues, and not the sort that has a man wanting to be with her." He laughed and told her he agreed with her. "I'm Amarizi Auburn, but I prefer to be called Ama. I don't know my father, and my mother is.... I'm an earth faerie, or so this man told me a few years ago. I have a job working in a pizza place for Peter Gunn."

He had heard of faeries but not any sort of specific kind. "And what exactly is an earth faerie, and what is the mark on your face?"

"I can control things that are earthbound. Not a lot of them are very useful or else I'm not very good at them yet, but Jacob told me that I'd get the hang of it with practice. He said.... What is it?"

"Jacob the wizard?" She nodded, and he felt the air rush from his lungs. "He was here last year. My sister-in-law and brother Dylan helped him with something. He told me...he said that you...he said that my mate was coming soon. I thought he meant like then, but.... Christ, he told me that you'd be more than I'd ever hope for."

"I'm not going to be your mate. Never. Whatever magic I hold now is too much. I don't want any more." She stood up and so did he. "I want to go back to my job now. If you won't let your brother take me, I'll call a cab."

"I'm sorry, but.... Do you know what will happen if another male touches you? I will kill them. And you and I are going to be mates whether you want it or not. I'm not saying that to piss you off, but it's fated that you and I are together." He didn't tell her that he wanted it as well, and figured he'd live longer if he didn't. "Look, I'll take you back to work. I don't like it, but I know right now that you're stressed and I don't want you hurting like this."

He moved to the sink, pulled down a travel glass for her, filled it with the rest of the cold tea, and handed it to her. He needed to touch her, and if this was the only way, then he'd do it this way. When she reached for the glass, he thought she was going to take it and disappoint him, but she looked up at him as her fingers were inches from his hand.

"Touching me without permission is certain death for you. Telling anyone, and I mean anyone, what I am is death for you as well. But if I allow you...if you touch me now, as you want, then you'll see me for what I am and not like you see me now." She looked at his hand then at him again. "You'll be able to see me like I truly am, which is more than even your parents can. Their touch was an accident. I would give you permission so that you can see the monster that I am. It will change your mind about wanting me, I'm sure. Do you want that?"

What she was saying frightened him on so many levels. Seeing her? What did that mean, and what was he going to see? Without thinking any more about it, he lifted his finger from the glass and ran it along her outstretched hand, and felt the power from her as it moved up his fingers to his body. Christ, she wasn't just powerful, she was electrifying.

~~~

She watched his face as he moved his fingers along her hand and up her arm where she'd pulled up her sleeve. He never took his eyes from hers, and she could see each emotion he had as he touched her. Each bit of magic that ran up his fingers and into him.

"Your skin is very soft and warm. Do you run hot?" His question had all sorts of images popping into her mind, most of which had to do with them both being naked and sweaty sheets, and he seemed to know it. "I'm betting that I'm making you hotter right now. The thought of seeing how hot you can really get has me hard as stone."

She glanced down without thinking and saw that his cock was indeed hard, and as she watched him it seemed to swell more. When she looked back up at him his eyes were closed, and she watched as he licked his lips. Every cell in her body seemed to heat up more.

"I can smell you." He moaned. "You're aroused, and I would like nothing more than to press my body against yours."

She wanted to pull away but couldn't. As his fingers moved along her elbow then up over her sleeve, she waited to see where he'd touch her next. She'd never known that having someone touch her like he was would feel so erotic.

When he pressed his thumb over the pulse at her throat she moaned.

"I want to kiss you, Ama. May I?" His voice was silky smooth and so husky that she found herself wanting him to do just that. As his head moved toward hers, she licked her own lips and watched as he got closer and closer to her. When his mouth brushed gently against hers, he leaned in more. But before she could touch her mouth to his for the promised kiss, she felt something she'd never felt before and pulled away.

"There's something at the front door." He felt her stiffen, and another low growl came from him. She took a step back, then another. She was both glad and very sad that he let her go. She moved to the door that the others had moved through just as Khan was going to the front door to open it.

"Don't." He stopped and looked at her. She heard Sebastian come up behind her but didn't look at him. "Something is out there."

Khan nodded and took a step back when she moved in front of him. Sebastian put his hand on her arm and turned her to him so that he was whispering in her ear.

"You said something, not someone. Is it dangerous enough that we should simply not answer?"

She looked up at him. *"He knows I'm here."* When he started to push her behind him, she grabbed his arm. *"I'm stronger than him, but he knows that you're going to answer the door. I'm not really sure what he is, but he plans to kill anyone that answers that's not me. You'll need to…. Can you trust me?"*

"With my life." She hadn't expected that and she was sure he knew it. *"We're going to have to talk, Ama. The fact that you can speak to me like this and know something is out there is enough for me to know that we're fated to be together."*

51

She didn't answer but moved to the door after motioning for Khan to step back. She didn't touch the door but opened it, staying back about a foot. She looked at the creature there, knowing that she was seeing him for what he was and not what he was trying to project.

"You're to come with me, mistress. I have been sent by one stronger than you to bring you to him." He bowed before her. "I am but a servant to him, so would ask that you not kill me."

"A messenger, not a servant, and one that is too weak for me to bother with. You do not serve him in any way other than as a profit to yourself. Don't lie to me again." He looked at her, then dropped his head again. "Who sent you and for what purpose?"

"As I have said, simply to bring you to him. And I cannot say his name without permission." She nodded. "Will you come with me and bring your mate?"

"I will not." She reached out into his mind and found nothing but an order to bring her to him, and the mate she had recently taken. "And you're mistaken in thinking I have a mate. I have no one that I've bonded with."

She felt Sebastian move up behind her, but he didn't touch her. Khan was close as well, and the others were coming, too. She had no idea what they would feel about her, but she had to send a message back to the one who'd sent this being.

"You know what I am?" He nodded and smiled. Evil poured from his lips in the form of a mist, and she raised her hand to stop it. "You've pissed me off. Do you know what happens now?"

He took a step back, and then another as her power stretched out to grab him. He was struggling to get away as she wrapped strong bands around his throat. She heard the men behind her and tried to ignore them. The being in front of her had her full attention.

"You've lied again. You've no idea what I am. But I know what you are." She tightened the bands more and watched him shift and twist. As soon as she was sure he was going to become real to the men behind her, she raised her other hand to protect them.

His body shifted again, and he became real. "You've made a mistake, mistress. He'll know what you are as soon as I go back to him. Then we shall see what happens to your precious mate."

"Kill him." The words whispered through her mind. *"Kill him now before he gives the other the information."*

She pushed power into him, and he screamed out in pain. As soon as he began to tremble in her grip, she pushed harder and he exploded. Mist, black as his evil, rained onto the porch. With a wave of her hand, the fragments of his body blew away.

Ama turned back to the men and saw that the women, Monica and Corrine, had joined them. They were all looking at her with the most shocked faces she'd ever seen. There was no way she could explain what had just happened, wasn't sure she wanted to. She walked to the kitchen, picked up her purse, and moved out of the house before anyone could tell her to leave. She was nearly to the turn-out driveway when someone stepped up beside her.

"May I ask where you're going?" She glanced at Sebastian and told him she was going to work. "If you'll give me a minute to get my keys, I'll take you."

"No thanks. I need to walk." He handed her the glass of tea he'd made for her earlier, and she took it. "Thank you. I'll make sure you get it back."

"This isn't over, Ama. I don't know what you did back there, but I have a feeling that you just saved my family. I'd like to take you to work, then pick you up afterwards so we can have a talk."

"I told you before that there can't be anything between us. And as far as that demon went, he won't bother you again. I promise." He nodded. "I'm sorry you had to see that."

"I'm not." He pulled her to him and held her. "I'm just sorry you had to deal with him...or whatever it was."

As much as she wanted to be held by him, she knew that she didn't want this any more than he did. Pulling away, she moved toward the end of their drive and was walking along the sidewalk when he pulled up beside her in his car. When she kept moving, he got out of the driver's side, leaving his car running in the street, and came up on the sidewalk beside her. Car horns started beeping right away.

"You're going to get arrested." He shrugged and continued walking with her. "What are you doing? Are you trying to piss me off?"

"Will you do to me what you did to that being?" He grinned at her. "If so, then no, I'm not. I'm just trying to take you to work."

Horns continued beeping, and she was so embarrassed that she went to his car to get in. He beat her and opened the door for her. As soon as he was in his side, they started moving.

"This doesn't change anything. I'm still not going to see you after this. You can find some other panther, a nice one that will take you on. I don't have the time."

He nodded, and when they pulled up in front of Gunn's Pizza, she got out without another word. Before she was inside, he yelled her name.

"I'll be right here when you get off. And if you think to avoid me, I'll hunt you down. You owe me at least an explanation of what that was." She nodded and went inside, knowing that there was no hope for it. He'd keep at her until she told him everything.

Chapter 5

Sebastian went back to his store. He wasn't sure what time Ama got off, but figured a quick call to Peter to ask him would give him all the information he needed. He also decided to have a cleaning crew hit his house pretty hard. He'd been too busy lately to do much more than toss his dirty dishes in the dishwasher.

As soon as he entered his office, he saw Jacob the wizard sitting there.

"She's amazing, isn't she?" Sebastian sat down without answering him. "I told you the last time I was here that she was coming to change things for you."

"Yes, you did. But you said nothing about whatever that was that was at my brother's house being a part of it." Jacob had the good grace to drop his head. "What the hell was that thing anyway?"

"A demon. Well, actually, he was a lesser demon. Not worth much other than to take messages and pick things up. He wouldn't have been able to take her directly to his master, but he would have hurt her all the same." Jacob smiled at him. "He didn't tell his boss where she was, so in turn, he doesn't know where you are either."

"But he knows that I'm her mate." Jacob nodded. "How does he know that already? I've not so much as kissed her yet and he's coming to —"

"You've not kissed her even?" Jacob seemed so surprised by that that Sebastian was nervous. "You've touched her though, correct? I mean, there would be no way for him to find you if you hadn't touched her at least."

"I've touched her arm, and I might have brushed my mouth over hers. What the hell does that have to do with anything?" And why did Jacob's smile make him feel like he was being laughed at. "What's going on?"

"She's an earth faerie. And she's not the last of her kind, though your mom and dad believe her to be. The one who wants her can breed with her, and that's why he wants her. It's all very complicated. He can't claim her once you do. If you wish to claim her. Do you?"

"She keeps telling me no. I can't take her against her will no matter how much I want her." Sebastian tried to muddle through what he was being told. "You say he can't claim her once I have, yet he thinks I've already done so. Am I to assume that he thinks I've claimed her because you told him I have?"

"Oh no, I can't lie to him any more than I can Amarizi or you. She's very powerful. Actually, I think she's considered by most to be all that and a bag of chips, as your generation says."

Sebastian had never said that in his life, but he knew the reference. He sat up straighter in his chair and looked at Jacob for several minutes before speaking. He had to figure this out now so that when he picked up Ama from work he'd have intelligent questions to ask her.

"What is an earth faerie?" A book suddenly appeared on his desk, and he moved back from it when it suddenly opened up and began flipping through the pages.

"Some say that they were created to care for the earth for all time. See that picture?"

Sebastian nodded at the drawn picture once the book stopped moving. Before he could ask anything about the man and woman on the page who looked similar to what he'd seen Ama look like, the pages were turning again.

"Others think she's a daughter to one of the Fates. Not able to say whether or not that one is true, because one just doesn't ask." Sebastian nodded, not sure what the hell he was talking about. "A few gainsayers say that earth faeries are simply that, faeries of the Earth."

The book stopped again and there was another drawing. He put his hands on the pages so that he'd be able to look at it without it changing. The faerie looked just like Ama, except in this drawing she looked more…well, more of everything.

"A mated earth faerie." Sebastian looked up at him. "That's what they look like after they've mated. And she is everything people, all the people, think she is. Except for the daughter part. I honestly don't know the answer to that one."

The drawing showed her with streams of light coming from her fingers, and her hair glowed as well. Her sigil was more pronounced, larger across her face than even when he'd seen her in the kitchen. And this faerie had wings, wide and longer than her body. They seemed to be translucent, and also in this picture she was naked, with only a few leafs to cover her breasts and the juncture at her thighs.

"She said that you told her that she would come into her power once she mated." Jacob nodded at him sadly. "This is what she doesn't want. Not the extra power or me. She said she hates what she is and won't become my mate because of it."

"She said much the same to me when I told her about herself all those years ago. Then she didn't know what she was; only that she was going to become more powerful than anyone when she did." Jacob laughed slightly. "She is very stubborn and will give you a run for your money, I believe."

Sebastian silently agreed. When he lifted his hands, the book began to move again. This time it went only a few pages before it stopped. The faerie lay on dark ground with what appeared to be blood around her, and her wings were gone. There was also a dagger sticking from her chest. He looked up at Jacob when he realized this was a male faerie.

"Her father. I knew him long ago before this, obviously. He was a good man. He had great ideas for keeping this world clean and safe. It's what got him killed before Amarizi was born. Her mother died of a broken heart, never able to tell his daughter what they were."

It was suddenly too much. The book closed and disappeared before Sebastian was able to form a question. And when he did, he watched Jacob's face. He had told him he couldn't lie to him. He hoped that was true.

"She's an earth faerie and my mate, but she won't mate with me; so what will happen to her if this man, the demon, finds out?" Jacob looked away and Sebastian knew that his answer wasn't going to come without some information that he didn't want. "Jacob, tell me."

"She's going to die by her own hand, because she won't submit to him. And he'll need her to submit or her powers won't help him. You see, as an earth faerie the females carry most of the power and when they mate, the power is shared. But the bond must be freely given. Somewhat like the pledge given to your mate." Jacob got up to pace around the small room. "Her father had been tricked into a deal. Not lied to but tricked. When he lost, the demon was to have his first-born child. When payment was to be made and the demon demanded his first-born, Amarizi's father said that he would not pay. When the demon came to her father for the babe seconds before his daughter was born, the demon, in a fit of rage, destroyed him. Her father lay dying as Amarizi was being brought into the world. As soon as she took her first breath, her father sent her all his love and all of his power. All of it."

"And that was a great amount, I'm assuming." Jacob smiled and nodded. "And you had to tell her what she was, and I guess you had to explain to her what these powers meant to her."

"No. I wish now that I had, but I was called away before I could help her with a little training, some control I guess. When I was able to return to her, she'd already changed and it was too late for me to talk to her then. She was too powerful for me."

"So you left her to fend for herself." Jacob nodded. "And that was supposed to help her how? And if you ask me, I think she has a great deal more control over this thing than I bet you think she does. Or even that thing that came to my brother's house thought she'd have."

"She would have gotten that from her father. He was, as I've said, very powerful as well. But there is something else you should know about the man who is trying to capture her. He isn't just a demon, but a great one. If he gets her into his lair, he will breed with her and in turn, she will kill herself. The death of the last female of her kind will be a great loss to all mankind."

And to me was all that Sebastian could think about. Jacob paced some more, and Sebastian ignored him for the most part. She was his mate, and if he didn't figure out some way for her to come to him willingly, she would end up with the demon that wanted her and die. When Jacob said his name, he looked up at him.

"She will need her strength to beat him. If you can't give it to her, I must find her another that can. She will not like it, but I'll simply make her love another so that she will come into full power. She can't survive without it."

The thought of her going to another made him growl. His cat moved along his skin like he wanted out to kill the man who dared try to take what was his. Sebastian stood up and stretched to let his cat know that he'd take care of this. Moving to Jacob, he watched fear roll through his eyes and was happy for it.

"You even think those words again and you'll wish for the demon to kill you, understand?" Jacob nodded and opened his mouth to speak. Sebastian cut him off. "Let me talk with her tonight. I'll let you know when I've convinced her that she needs me more than I need her."

"Good luck, Sebastian. I believe you'll need it." As he left, Sebastian was pretty sure Jacob was right. He was going to need a great deal more than luck to win this woman's hand. He made his way to his desk again after Jacob left. His first call was to the cleaning crew to come out, the second to the pizza place where Ama worked.

"Peter, I was wondering if you can help me with a little romance problem I have." Peter laughed at him and Sebastian smiled. "Your dishwasher is my mate, and she seems to think she can tell me that she won't want me."

"You should know that she's a bit stronger than you. Her power...I've never met a...her kind before, and I know them to be strong, but this girl is off-the-charts strong." Sebastian remembered seeing on one of the pages of the book that you couldn't say what she was until she gave you permission. She'd obviously not given it to Peter.

"I know what she is and how strong she is, but what I don't know is how to convince her that I want her in my life. She seems to think that she can simply say no and that I'll say okay." He laughed a little. "I hate when I'm told no when I want something."

"You might live longer if you just walk away from her if she continues to tell you no." The laughter from the big bear made him think Peter was going to help him. "I'll talk you up. She wants me to call her a cab when I'm about ready to shut the place down. Want maybe I should call you? You know, you could sort of be her ride, so to speak."

"That would be very helpful and yes, I'd be very happy to give her a ride home. Thanks." He thought about the apartment that he thought she'd been about to move into, and asked Peter to tell her that it had been rented.

"I can't lie to her. I don't know what it is about her that forbids it, but anyone who speaks to her can't lie to her." Sebastian knew that, but wasn't sure if he'd realized it meant that no one could lie to her.

After making sure that Peter knew how to contact him, he hung up. He knew that things weren't moving into place really, but they were moving in the right direction. He went home to let the crew in. Sebastian said he'd pay them a bonus if they got it cleaned before midnight. He hoped they had enough time.

~~~

Her feet hurt more than she could have imagined they would. As she moved to the front of the shop to leave, she noticed that Peter was talking to someone. When he moved into the light, she saw who it was. Damn it all to hell.

"What the hell are you doing here?" Sebastian grinned at her. "I'm going home in a cab or walking, but not with you."

"I'm not taking you to your apartment." She wasn't sure what she was missing, but was sure it was something when he grinned more. "Come on, I've got my car all warmed up for you."

"I thought you just said you weren't taking me home." He stood near his car and waited for her as they came out. "I'm really tired and just want you to leave me alone."

"I can feel how tired you are. And I can also feel your hunger. You come with me and I'll feed you a thick steak and baked potato. I also think there might be a piece of strawberry shortcake in your future if you'll be a good girl and eat all your dinner."

There was something very appealing about him when he was teasing. She tried to ignore the thought of steak and potato and strawberry shortcake, but her belly was singing to her to go with the man and feed it. She stood next to him and stared up at him.

"You're not going to try and convince me that I should be your mate, are you?" He just stared at her. "I want you to answer me."

"I can't lie to you. And if I can't lie to you, I don't want to piss you off with the truth. How's that for an answer?" She opened the door herself and got into the passenger seat. When he went around the car and got in, she wanted to touch him but knew that she couldn't.

"Why are you doing this?" He looked at her like he was confused. "Why do you care if I eat or not? It can't matter to you if I'm hungry or not."

"A great many things about you matter to me." He handed her a large travel glass, and she took a sip and moaned. He glanced at her as he drove out of the lot. He was getting onto the highway when he started talking.

"Why sweet?" She looked at him. "Why do you need sweet stuff when you're stressed? I mean, I think it's great, but I would have thought maybe juice or something like that."

"I love juice, but it's terribly expensive. Not to mention most of the stuff you buy is little more than sweetened water with a little juice added in anyway. I love tea, especially the kind that has flavors in it."

"I like raspberry tea myself, and have some at home now. We'll have some with dinner." He drove a little more and she had just closed her eyes when he spoke again. "I had a visitor today. Jacob came to see me."

She sat up so quickly that she nearly spilled her tea. Her heart was pounding so hard that she knew he could hear it. When he reached for her hand, she let him curl his fingers around hers without thinking. She looked at him as her body started to calm.

"I don't suppose he told you that he found a way to remove this stuff from me, did he?" She felt his shock. "I asked him to look for a way. I had hoped he'd come to me sooner."

"I don't think...he didn't mention it. He did tell me about the demon that came to the house today. He said that if his master finds you and brings you back to his lair, he will try and breed with you." She felt him look at her as the car pulled to a stop in a driveway. "Did he tell you that?"

"No. He told me about what I was and that my powers would grow once I took a mate." She looked out the side window and not at him. "I don't want to mate with anyone, not just you. It's too dangerous for me to be around real people now. I can't imagine what it would be like if I had a mate."

"I would think you'd be safer with a mate." She didn't say anything to that, not sure what she'd say anyway. "How about we go inside and I feed you? I'm not a great cook, but I can cook a really good steak. The potatoes should be about done by now."

She got out and followed him to his door. She couldn't see much as it was very dark out here in the forest. His house was large and white and that was about all she could make out as he opened the door to the kitchen. Ama stepped into his house and nearly fell over.

"It's beautiful. And I love this kitchen." She walked around the room looking at all the counter space and the smaller appliances that he had spaced around. She loved the refrigerator that was a huge side-by-side with glass front doors, and the cabinets that seemed to glow with the lights behind the beveled glass on them. She walked to the stove and fell in love with the gas-top burners and the large grill in the middle. She laughed when she thought of all the dinners that must get made here.

"I'm going to confess something to you. This place was a sty up until about an hour ago. I've been really busy at work and trying to balance the two jobs I have, and had sort of neglected this place for a while. You have the best cleaning crew I've ever seen to thank for this being clean." She nodded and took the glass of tea he handed her. "There's more in the fridge. Just help yourself. I'm going to go out and fire up the grill for our dinner. How do you want yours cooked?"

She told him rare, and he smiled at her. He told her if she wanted salad that it was on the second shelf, to make them each a bowl. She pulled out the large bowl as he stepped outside.

By the time the steaks were done, he'd shown her where to find plates and silverware as well as the dressings. She was putting the warm rolls on the table when he brushed against her while putting the steaks on their plates. She felt as if he'd touched her everywhere. Nervous, she backed up as he turned to her.

"I won't hurt you." She nodded, knowing that he would anyway. "I'd very much like to kiss you again. This time without interruptions. May I?"

Ama wanted to tell him no, that it wasn't a good idea, but he put the platter he had the steaks on into the sink, along with his utensils. He took a step toward her and she didn't back away, as was her habit. When he was just inches from her, she looked up at him and licked her lips.

"Do you have any idea what you're doing to me? How it feels to be this close to you without touching you?" He touched her throat in the barest of touches and then cupped his hand behind her head. "I need this from you. May I please kiss you?"

"Yes," was barely out of her mouth when he sealed his lips over hers. He tilted her head to his left and ran his tongue along her sealed lips, asking for permission to enter her. When she opened her mouth slightly, he took her hungrily and she moaned and reached for something to hang onto. It just happened to be his shirt.

As his tongue slid along hers, she moved her hands up his chest to his shoulders. He ran his free hand down her back to her ass and cupped her against him. She felt his hardness against her and moved, thinking to pull back. But as soon as she felt his cock at her soft folds, she gripped him harder across his shoulders and moaned against this mouth. She was clinging to him even as he lifted her off the floor.

Something hard touched her back, and she moaned again when his body pressed deeper into hers. Wrapping her arms around his shoulders, he lifted her leg up by her thigh and she wrapped her legs around him without thought as to what she was doing and where this was going to end up. His mouth moved along her chin to her throat, and she tilted her head for him, giving him whatever he needed to bring them to wherever he needed. Her body was screaming at her to touch him like he was touching her, and she nuzzled her nose against his pounding pulse, suckled the vein into her mouth, and nipped at him.

"Christ, I want you. I need you." Her shirt was torn from her and his mouth was everywhere. Her breasts were suddenly freed, and his mouth was covering them.

"Please." She didn't know what she needed, but he apparently did because he rocked into her again and again. "More please. I need more."

He lifted his head. She looked at him, on the verge of begging him to finish her, when she saw his eyes. They had darkened from the warmed honey color to the dark of his panther. She nipped at his chin, and he moaned at her.

"Give it to me. We can't go any further until you tell me I can." Her mind was trying to understand him. Then he lifted her chin up again when she tried to go back to his throat. "I want you, but you need to give me permission to do this."

Permission. She'd forgotten about that, and stared at him as he waited for her answer. He would take her and make her his if she said yes. And as much as she wanted to feel him, to have him take her, she didn't want all that came with it. She felt him as he began to pull away.

"I'm sorry, Sebastian. I can't be your mate." He nodded as he stepped back. "Maybe you should just take me home."

"I can't until we eat. It's probably cold by now, so if you want something else just let me know."

She went to the table and sat down. Her legs were trembling, and she figured if she didn't, she was going to fall.

"Let me make you something else. It won't be a problem."

"It's fine. It's still warm and since we didn't unwrap the potatoes, they're still warm, too." Opening the aluminum foil, she watched as steam poured from it. "See, it's just fine."

He sat down and opened his foil and looked up at her. She was just about to speak but looked at his neck and froze. There was blood there. She'd bitten him. She went to him and ran her finger over the opened wound.

"I marked you." Dizzily, she reached for the table and missed. As she dropped to the floor, she heard him say her name, and as the darkness closed around her, she knew that it was too late for either of them.

Chapter 6

Wanera paced his lair and reached again for his messenger. Nothing. It was as if he was blocking him. And Wanera knew that he couldn't do that any more than he could think a thought that he hadn't given him. The man was simply a being that took messages to and fro for him.

He glanced at the file on his desk and sneered at it. Since it had been brought to him, he'd been having one problem after another. And now this. His messenger was to go and get the girl and bring her back here. He should have returned hours ago, but still nothing.

"Where the fuck are you?" He had nearly decided to go to the upper world and get her himself when he heard a small scratching at the door. "Come in, and whatever you want, it had better be fucking important."

The door opened slowly, and the being there seemed to be terrified nearly to the point of bolting. Wanera told him if he left without telling him what he'd disturbed him for, he'd hunt him down and vanquish him.

"He's here, my lord. Your messenger has been returned to us." Wanera started forward and was on the verge of asking why the messenger didn't come there himself when the being swallowed before continuing. "He's been returned, my lord, and reeks of faerie."

Wanera stopped. The being had said "been" returned, not that he'd returned. Wanera felt a bit of fear trickle along his skin as he thought about what the implications were to what the being was saying. The thought "returned" kept circling around in his head.

"Who returned him?" The being shrugged. "Where is he now? And what, if anything, did he bring back with him?"

"He is in the main hall, my lord, the point he left this realm from. And he brought nothing back with him but the smell of female faerie. What shall I do with his remains?"

No body, but remains. He started to tell the being to throw the remains in one of the pits, but thought he'd better take care to see if he might have brought something back with him. Wanera told the being to take him to the remains and show them to him. He didn't know what to expect, but when he saw what had been done to the body, he nearly grabbed for a wall. She had destroyed him.

There was really no way other than smell to know that the pieces on the floor had belonged to him. The messenger had been with Wanera for a very long time, decades as a matter of fact, but to see this mess now it was hard to think of it as a person he once knew. He knelt down and sniffed. Faerie, and one not as young as he'd been led to believe.

"Where did he come from, can you tell?" The being said that he could not. "I must know where he found her, and go and make her repay me for what she's taken from me."

"I cannot, my lord, other than to tell you that he was in the world of humans. I could try to trace him back, but there is very little of him left to go by. Sometimes I can search a mind of a body, but this.... This, sire, I cannot."

Wanera nodded. He looked at the pieces and wondered how she'd killed him so easily. The messenger belonged to him and thus had some powers of protection, but the faerie that had killed like this had been very strong.

"When you told me you'd found a faerie on the upper worlds, I thought you said she was no more than a child in my lifetime. The one that did this is a good deal older than a mere child, I think." The being simply nodded. "Are you saying that you agree with me, or that she was a child?"

"Both, my lord. When you had me look for a female faerie, I told you that they might well be extinct. An older one, many years older than even you, died some years back. I mentioned that there might have been another that showed up, but it disappeared and I thought it dead as well. Then when a few weeks ago one came up on my screen, I only thought her to be young, as she had not come fully into herself."

Meaning that he thought she'd not hit her maturity yet. But the one that had done this had most assuredly been mature. The being had walked away to his computer and was keying in information. When Wanera asked him what he was doing, he said he was looking for the faerie.

"She would have left a magical trail behind after using the amount of magic needed to do this. I am trying to find it. I can only think that it had to have happened within the last twenty-four to forty-eight hours." As he continued to put in more information, Wanera leaned against the other desk.

"I thought that all beings were to be returned to me immediately. How did this happen so long ago and he's just now being returned to me?" The being shrugged. "Do you know anything?"

"Yes, sire, I know plenty, but never as much as you." The answer sounded like he'd been practicing it, but before he could question him on it, the being turned in his chair. "She is young and powerful, my lord. So much so that she's able to keep her magic to a low hum. I can find a bit of a trail, but it is so small that I cannot know if she used it on this messenger or at another time. I could send something there to check and—"

"I'll go. I want to see firsthand where she's at." The being nodded and turned back to his desk. "When will I be able to be—?"

The alley he was standing in was dark and wet smelling. He looked around the area and tried to find something, anything other than the nasty smell of humans that seemed to permeate the air like a disease. Then as he was ready to call to come home, he smelled something. It wasn't faerie but.... "Panther."

He shivered when he thought of weres. They were the most vicious group of beings ever created. He hated panthers more than he did anything else. They were sleek and dark, and were the only beings he'd ever encountered that could take him down—and once had.

It was just after he'd gone to collect the child he'd been promised. Fryda and his mate Pendus had been the only couple that he'd ever known that had bred. Their child had been due that week, and Fryda had lost a bet. Of course, the bet had been a trick—a lie actually, on Wanera's part—but he'd gone to a great deal of trouble to get the babe and Fryda had said no.

Killing him had drained him. A being so powerful had nearly killed him in the process, but when Wanera had severed Fryda's wing from his body, he seemed to fall apart. Wanera had never known that a faerie could be killed after their maturity, and he'd done it all by himself.

But he hadn't been able to get the child. The mate, Pendus, had just given birth, yet she was as powerful, if not more so, than her mate. When she'd raised her hand against him, Wanera had done the only thing he could do and left the house to go back to his own lair to heal. It had taken him nearly five years to heal, not able to make his wounds close until he had finally taken a hot blade to them and closed them off. He rarely looked at the huge, ugly scars on his legs and chest anymore. But the panther that had given the worst ones to him had died that night, too.

He'd come out of nowhere, his fangs dripping with saliva. As Wanera stood over the body of Fryda, the panther looked at Wanera as though he knew that he'd killed Fryda. The panther had leapt at him, tearing a large opening across his chest as his claws connected with his flesh. As Wanera had tried to stand up and leave the magical realm, the panther had attacked again, this time tearing a large opening in his thigh. Bone was exposed, and his muscles were torn so badly that he still couldn't walk for long before the pain got to be too much. Killing the panther had proven to be nearly as hard as the faerie, and by the time Wanera had returned to his bed, he was nearly dead, too. Without the help of his beings, he would have perished long ago.

As he moved closer to the scent of the panther, he could smell traces of the female. Humans had been with her as well as several panthers. One of them was a male, the leader of his group. He moved to the opening of the alley and called to return home. He'd found no traces of his messenger there.

"Keep looking," he told the being as soon as he returned to his lair. "That wasn't where he died. And the next time you send me off like that without some warning, I will come back here and make your remains look worse than that one." He pointed to the mess being cleaned up from the front hall. "And make sure that you take him to be buried. He served me long enough to reap that benefit."

Wanera paced his lair. Fire blazed hot in this room and would have roasted a large elk had he any desire for food. But he needed the warmth now that he'd returned from the human world. Something in the other world always made him ill and chilled to the bone. He flopped himself into his chair and tried to think.

He needed the faerie more than he needed anything else right now. He glanced at the large tome over the mantel. He'd forgotten about the curse that had come to him when he'd taken this job. He had to find a female to breed with and have a child before the next summer solstice. If he did not, then he would be killed and his replacement would do it. He could have a child of his own take over for him once he was mature enough to do it, and watch over him as he grew into his power, but he had to have the child or have one expected to be born before the summer. That gave him less than one year to find her, be given her permission to take her, and to breed her. Not going to be easy to say the least. He reached for the book near him and opened it to a random page.

Romance was not his cup of tea. Snarling at the words on the pages, Wanera thought it dribble and trite that any person would have to go through something as stupid as a wooing ritual to lure a woman into his bed. He thought that simply taking what he wanted should be enough, and that any female should be impressed with his ability to fuck her so well and so thoroughly and to breed with her. He didn't think that this faerie was going to be that easy.

But he no longer had a choice. He needed to have a being much like himself— which he was sad to admit had eluded him until they were all taken by others—or one as strong or stronger than him. The only thing stronger than him was the faerie and there was just the one left. The scratching at his door had him bidding them to enter.

"I have found a small trail, sire. I do not believe it to be from the same female, but there might be enough of her power to do what you need. She is in a place called New Mexico. Have you heard of it?" Wanera nodded and stood up. "She is there, and if you would give me your permission, I will send you there posthaste."

Wanera nodded once and felt the air stir. Then he was standing outside a door in a house with no idea what he was going to do. He was seriously going to have to figure out some ground rules for the beings he had working for him. Like, when he'd said yes, he had his permission to send him, he'd hoped that the being would at least give him the chance to ask a few questions so he'd be somewhat prepared. Apparently, asking for it and receiving the okay meant to go fucking right now.

The door opened before he could knock. The male standing before him didn't look like he was human, much less faerie. He smiled at him, and the man raised a brow. This was not going to end in his favor, Wanera just knew it.

"I don't suppose you're a faerie, are you?" Steam seemed to pour from the male, and before Wanera could do much more than blink, the man had hit him, hard enough to knock him back onto his ass. He started to stand when the man came out of the room and stood, really towering over him.

"What my sexual preference is has no bearing on me, do you understand me?" Wanera nodded, not having a clue. "A man or woman has their rights just the same as straight people. Get the fuck away from here before I have my partner blow you to pieces."

The man standing behind the mammoth held a gun pointed right at Wanera's head. It wasn't loaded with silver, but at that moment, Wanera knew that he'd hurt him all the same. He called to his being and was on the floor of his offices seconds later. He didn't move as he looked up at his being.

"I want you to know that the next time you send me to the upper world without letting me be prepared, I will kill you." The being nodded. "And I need for you to look up the word faerie and what it has to do with sexual preferences."

"It has to do with gay relationships, sire. The slang for the people who are in same-sex relationships is called fairies. I do not believe it to be the same thing." Wanera only glared at him. "Did you find the faerie that you were looking for?"

Without answering him, Wanera stood up and went to his room. Stupid beings were going to be the death of him sooner or later. Pulling the small romance book to his lap, he started reading again the story of a female and her tribulations in trying to escape the arms of the one that wanted her, even though she wanted him as passionately as he wanted her. Passion was another word that made him ill. He forced himself to read until bedtime, then tossed it in the fire. Hopefully one of the hundreds of others would be of more use than that one had been.

~~~

Sebastian watched her sleep. He'd been so terrified when she fainted that he'd called for his entire family to come to him. His mom had been the first to answer his call. She was so calm that he felt himself relax more as she spoke.

"She will be fine, Sebastian. A person like her will heal quickly, and whatever it was that frightened her will be gone by the time she wakes." He doubted he'd leave her but told his mom he agreed. But when she asked him what had happened shortly before she'd fainted, he stumbled around on how to tell her.

"She bit me. Not that I noticed, but there was blood on my neck after we'd pulled apart. I didn't take her because I was told I need permission, but we'd gotten into heavy…she bit me on the neck and I nearly…Christ." She was laughing, and he felt his face heat up with embarrassment. "This isn't easy on me."

"I don't doubt it. If she took you first, then you've been given permission to take back, I would think. But I'm not sure. She's so much different than us." He wanted to agree with that whole heartedly, but only said that she was right. "You should have something for her when she wakes up. Something romantic. Do you have anything?"

He hadn't, but a quick trip to the woods behind his house provided that for him. He looked up at the large vase of flowers he'd picked for her. He'd wanted to give her chocolates and roses, but it was the best he could do and not leave her. There was no way he was leaving her now.

"Where am I?" He stood up when she spoke softly. Asking her if he could turn on the light, he did so and sat on the bed next to her.

"You fainted." She looked away from him. "You also bit me. Does that mean I can bite you back?"

He was half teasing with her, but she looked at him as if he was going to tear her throat out. Before he could tell her that he would never harm her, she sat up and put her finger over the tiny scar that had already formed there.

"Does it hurt?" He shook his head no. "I didn't even know that I'd done it until I saw the blood. I had hoped that you'd cut yourself shaving, but you didn't, did you?"

"No. You marked me." She shifted on the bed, and her breast brushed against his arm. She stilled, and he watched her. "You've marked me. Does that mean that we're bonded?"

He heard his question but had a hard time thinking that the voice that spilled from his lips was his. He'd heard his voice go husky before when trying to win a woman over to…he looked away from her and at the flowers.

"I got these for you." She didn't look at them but kept staring at him; he could feel her eyes as they took in all of him. When he turned to her, he pulled her to him and took her mouth. Need to mark her back was pulling his cat to the surface.

Her moan was his undoing. Had she pushed him away or pulled away, he might have been able to stop. But when she also wrapped her arms around him, he rolled over her and pressed her into the bed. He had to have her right now.

He tore at her ruined shirt and lifted her bra up as he made his way down her throat. Her taste was erotic, and he needed more. Shifting his body over hers, he settled between her legs and rocked into her.

"Answer me, Ama. Tell me that you've marked me and that I can mark you as well." She moaned again when he nipped hard at her nipple. "Tell me."

"Yes," she screamed out. "Yes, I've marked you and now you have my permission to mark me as well."

He didn't wait for her to change her mind, but rolled to his back and sat up. Her breasts were heaving and he wanted nothing more than to lean down and suckle at them until he came, but he wanted her fully and reached down and tore her jeans from her. Long legs, pale as the moon shining over them, moved under his stare, moving wider for him until he thought he'd die from the pleasure.

Rolling over her, he stood up at the side of the bed, pulled his shirt over his head, and dropped it to the floor. Next, he unsnapped his pants as he toed off his shoes. She watched him as hungrily as he watched her. Pulling his pants off, he stood before her naked, his cock straining to be buried deep within her heat. He ran his hand up and down his aching cock.

"I know you're a virgin so you'll hurt when I take you. I'm sorry for that." She nodded and reached for him. He let her touch him, and when she took the pearl drop of his precum onto her finger, he watched to see what she'd do with it. When she put her finger into her mouth, he had to stop what he was doing or he'd come all over her.

"You taste like your blood. Hot, spicy, and like I'd think you would." He watched her lick her lips, then move toward him again, this time with her mouth. He took a step back from her.

"You do that and I'll come down your throat. As much as I'd like to do that, coming inside of you is what I need more than anything." She nodded at him and lay back. "Christ, you're like a feast for me. I don't know where to start."

Her fingers curled into the sheet as she moved on the bed. "Come to me, please? I need you, all of you."

Sebastian dropped to his knees before her and took her breast into his mouth again. While he nibbled on her nipple, he ran his hand down her body to the juncture at her thighs. She nearly came up off the bed when he slid beneath her curls and into her. She was soaking wet.

Lifting his head, he watched her as he fucked her this way. Her body rode his fingers, and he realized that he wanted to taste her when she came the first time. Moving down her body, he kissed her and nipped at her flesh until he was where he wanted to be in the worst way. Lifting her leg up, he put it behind him and then turned her in the bed so that she was open for him. Lowering his head to where her scent was the strongest, he opened her lips and suckled her clit into his mouth as he slid deeper into her.

She screamed as she flooded his mouth. Her legs tightened around him so tightly that he was sure she was going to hurt him. Nipping at her again brought her to peak again, and he knew that if he entered her now that she'd not feel the pain of him taking her. Pulling her off the bed, he had meant to have her stand, but her pussy touched his cock, and he jerked her down over him before he could think.

Christ, he knew that he'd hurt her badly this time. Holding her without letting her pull away, he spoke to her softly. He had no idea what he was saying. Just words, stories of his childhood and things that he'd learned on the computer. When she raised her tear-stained face at him, he smiled back at her when she smiled at him.

"I'm sorrier than I've ever been for taking you this way. I only meant to give you as much pleasure as I could before I took your maidenhead. I can't tell you how horrible I—"

"Did you really get caught skinny dipping with a girl named Paula when you were ten?" He tried to think where she'd heard that when he realized that he'd told her. "I can't believe your mother didn't beat you within an inch of your life."

"She didn't actually, but told me that my dad would. When my dad took me out to the shed, he had a long talk with me about sex, and how as a panther I had to be careful, that girls were precious no matter what they were. I agreed, but wondered why anyone would want to have sex. He looked at me very strangely and asked me if that was what I'd been doing with Paula. I told him no, that she'd had a pool and it was hot."

She laughed, and he smiled again. Then she laid her head on his chest and he held her there. He needed to move soon or his knees were going to go out on him, but for now he was enjoying holding her.

"You didn't come, did you?" He shook his head. "You hurt me. I didn't think it would hurt that badly when I'd thought about sex at all."

"I didn't mean to take you this way. When I pulled you off the bed, I'd meant to…I'm not sure what I'd meant to do, but I needed to be inside of you, and I was jerking you around to take you. I'm profoundly sorry." She nodded. "I need to stand up, love. My knees are killing me."

She moved a little and his cock jerked inside of her. She looked up at him, and he nearly begged her to leap off him before he hurt her again, but then she wrapped her fingers into his hair and rolled her hips over him. He moaned.

"You keep that up and I'm going to roll you to the floor and finish what we started." Her hips rose and lowered again when she wrapped her legs around him. "Ama, I'm not kidding. I'm so close to taking you that I ache."

"Then take me. Now, Sebastian. Please? Take me." He lifted her closer to his body and stood on one foot. Her body seemed to stretch to take more of him in. He nearly threw her to the bed then, but he needed to at least get off his knees. Standing up, he held her to him and took her mouth. He moved slowly toward the wall opposite of them while all the time lifting and lowering her over him. By the time she was pressed against the wall, she was crying out her release and sinking her teeth into his throat. With a roar of his own, Sebastian let his canines drop as his cock exploded in her, and snapped his teeth into her shoulder.

Chapter 7

Ama sat at the table and watched the steam curl off the top of her cup. She didn't care for hot tea normally, but she needed something to do with her hands and the tea bags had fallen out of the cabinet when she'd been reaching for a glass to have a glass of tea. Making the tea had been somewhat relaxing, but now that she was done she didn't know what to do.

She was mated to a panther. Gently touching the scar at her shoulder, she shivered at the sensations it created. He was her mate. They had had sex twice more after he'd put her to bed. Both times had left her limp and so sated that she doubted that she'd ever move again. But he'd touch her and she'd be ready again. She had just gotten up to use the bathroom and found her way down here about an hour ago. She looked down at her arms and wondered what the rest of her looked like.

When she'd used his bathroom, she avoided looking in the mirror. It wasn't hard to do. She'd been doing it for years, but her arms were something that she could see without the aid of a mirror. And the change in them was amazing.

The webbing no longer moved along her skin but seemed to have filled it. Now instead of the crossing marks on her skin, there was an almost sheer undertone to them in a shade of the palest green she'd ever seen. And it seemed to sparkle. She had a moment to wonder what a human would see if they saw her now, and pushed that thought to the back of her mind. She was sure she didn't want to know.

"Are you all right?" Startled, she turned to look at him, and he smiled at her. "I reached for you and you were gone and I panicked. Are you okay?"

"I'm not sure I will be ever again." He grinned bigger at her. "That's not what I meant. I meant that now that we've done this, I'm not sure what happens now."

He sat down across from her and noticed the tea. "Do you normally drink hot tea? I do sometimes but not often. If you'd like I can get you one of those brewers. I've been thinking about it for some time."

"I never drink it. But I needed something to do." He nodded and stood up to get a glass and ice. He dumped her now warm tea over the ice and handed it back to her. "Thank you. I think I'll like this better."

"You never answered me. Are you okay?" She took a sip of the tea and nodded. "You don't act like it. Are you sorry we did this?"

"No," she answered him immediately. "Never this. I'm afraid but I don't regret it. Do you? Regret this, I mean."

"Never." He stood up and went to his refrigerator and started setting things on the counter. "I'm starved. How about you? We didn't get any dinner last night. I don't know about you, but I worked up quite an appetite."

She stood up, walked up behind him, and wrapped her arms around his waist. He turned in her arms and pulled her tightly against him. She felt the tears threaten as he ran his fingers up and down her back.

"We're a couple now and you're going to become more powerful. Is that what you're afraid of?" She nodded against his chest. "I'm not. I know that whatever happens now will only make us more of what we already are. I'm not afraid of this."

"You're going to have what I have." She felt his chuckle and looked up at him. "You might be marked like me. What will your brothers say then?"

"Congratulations? I think they'll be happy for us. In fact, I know they will." He pulled her back from him slightly. "And as for the marks, I think that's already started."

She stepped back, and he lifted the sleeve of his shirt and showed her the webbing curls of lines on his shoulder. His were as dark and detailed as hers were, with the same diamond pattern. She had him turn around, and she lifted his shirt up and could see it starting there as well. When he turned around to face her again, she sat down in the chair.

"I have more, but you're changing. You're going to be like me soon." He asked her if he could see her back. "I've not looked at it in a very long time. Just after my birthday, I used to look daily. Now I try not to look."

She stood up and turned for him. When his breath touched her there, she felt her sigil move. Then his lips brushed over her and she felt her body tighten with need again. He skimmed his hands up and over her shoulders and down again before he kissed her along her spine.

"They're wings, aren't they?" She nodded at him as he took her breath away with each touch. "I think you're the most beautiful creature in the world, and you're all mine."

She moaned when he pulled her hips to his. His cock was hard and she moved back against him. He pulled her shirt over her head, and then her bra. He was pulling down her pants when she realized where they were and told him they could go upstairs.

"No, I want to take you in every room in this house, and then start all over when I'm finished. I want to enter any room and know that I've made you scream out my name while I pounded into you." She felt his cock and knew that he was as naked as she was. "Scream for me, Ama. I want to take you hard like this and have you scream out my name."

He leaned her over the table and entered her all in a smooth motion. He pressed her head to the table and she lay that way while he moved in and out of her slowly. She turned to look at him.

"You want me to scream, then you'd better do better than this." He laughed and rolled his hips so that he touched something deep within her. "I want to watch you while you fuck me. Please?"

He pulled out and helped her lay on the table. He moved between her legs and lifted them up to his shoulders. He was so deep that she could almost feel him in her throat. When she cupped her breasts and rolled her nipples, he stilled inside of her and she looked up at him.

"You want me to fuck you hard, you keep that up." She tweaked her nipple hard enough to make herself cry out. His cock jerked deep inside of her. "Again. Do it again and again until I come."

He watched her through hooded eyes as she played with her nipples. Soon he was pounding her hard enough that the table shook beneath her. When he dropped her legs down, she wrapped them around his hips and he leaned over her and took the nipple she offered him.

"Come." Her body responded immediately to his command and she screamed out her release as she grabbed for him. Pulling him down, she nipped at his shoulder and

Sebastian

then felt his teeth scrape along her throat. As soon as she cried out again, he bit her and she heard him roar against her throat as he drank from her. She reached for his shoulder and bit him as well; hot blood filled her mouth as she screamed out his name again and again.

The lights dimmed and the room seemed to shift beneath them. She knew he felt it, too, because he lifted his head to look down at her. He looked so concerned that she ran her fingers over the creases in his forehead. He kissed her quickly, then licked along the wounds at her throat.

"I should move off you." She wrapped her arms around him tighter. "I'm all for staying for the rest of the day, but I think if we don't have a meal soon, other than each other, one of my family members is going to come here looking for us and we're going to be locked together in a shriveled mess."

Reluctantly, she let him go. When he stood up, he gave her his hand and helped her to stand. Then when he asked her if she was all right several times, he went to the laundry room right off the kitchen and brought her back one of his shirts and a pair of his boxers. He'd slipped on a shirt and pants as well.

"You're going to have to bring your things here soon. I don't mind you wearing my clothes, but I'm pretty sure that you're going to get cold before winter hits." She felt a little odd nodding at his statement. "You are moving in here with me, right?"

"I don't know." He watched her as she washed her hands and began to put bacon in a skillet. "I don't know what to do. I know that we've mated and all that, but what happens when that man finds out where I am? I don't have the first clue how to keep you safe."

"You're not going to." She looked at him and he grinned at her. "We'll keep each other safe. It's the way we're going to

89

survive this. And according to Jacob, this guy can't take you so long as I'm your mate. So he'll have to look elsewhere for a person to have his children."

She was turning the bacon over when she looked up at him. "Do you really think that's the way it works? I mean, now all I need to do is tell him that I've taken another for my mate and he quits?"

"Probably not. But for now we're going to believe that while we have ourselves a big, unhealthy breakfast." He handed her a glass of tea. "And I'm going to have to go to the store to get more tea bags. You're drinking more than my family does on pizza night."

She knew he was kidding her, but she still flushed. When they sat down to eat, he handed her each platter before he took anything off it. She really was hungry and took a large part of each thing that they'd cooked.

"I'm stuffed." She leaned back in her chair thirty minutes later. "I don't think I'll eat ever again."

"You will. In about four hours. What's the plan for today?" She looked down at her borrowed clothes and then back up at him. "Right, clothes. And for your information, I think you're extremely sexy in my clothes."

They were headed to the "Y" when his cell phone rang, and she watched as he pulled over to answer it. He was getting tenser as whoever was on the other end continued to speak. She waited, knowing for some reason it was about her. When he closed his phone, he sat there for several seconds before he pulled back into traffic.

"That was Khan. He said that someone broke into one of the buildings we have downtown. He wants me to go and have a look at it." She nodded, wondering about the rest. When he didn't say anything, she finally turned to him.

"What else happened that you're not telling me?" He glanced at her. "I'm not stupid, so tell me."

"First of all, I never thought you were stupid. And the reason I didn't want to say anything is because what he wants me to look at might involve you. I can't tell you what it says, but he said that you're mentioned not by name but by reference. Khan is worried about you." She nodded and looked away. "Ama, they're not going to get you. None of us are going to let him take you." She nodded again, worried that it had begun so quickly after they had bonded.

~~~

Sebastian walked around the room where the most damage had been done. He thought he had seen his share of graffiti, but this was beyond anything he'd ever seen. Not only were the walls drawn on, but the floor as well. He glanced over at Ama, wondering if she could read what was written on the floor that had been squared off.

"You can." He jumped back when Jacob appeared before him. "You should use your new skills to know when I'm about. I wouldn't frighten you so badly if you did."

"New skills? I haven't the slightest idea what you're talking about." He glanced at Ama when she came toward them. "She's scared, so whatever this says and if it involves her, don't tell her."

"She will ask and I will tell." When she walked up to him and wrapped her arms around him, Sebastian felt he could take on the world. Jacob bowed before her. "My lady. Congratulations on your recent change."

"You should know that I'm slightly mad at you. You told me that you'd come back and help me. You didn't." He nodded at her and bowed again. "What does this all mean?"

Jacob looked at him and shrugged. Damn it, Sebastian had hoped she wouldn't notice the place he'd been wondering about. He nodded to Jacob, knowing that he was going to tell her anyway.

"Read it, you both can." Sebastian looked at him and wondered if the man had lost his mind. "You should know that you're projecting yourself very loudly, my lord. Anyone within a mile could hear you."

"I don't know what you mean." He had a feeling that the walls were closing in on him. "I'm feeling sort of strange."

He felt hands grab at him and he wanted to push them away, but a voice kept telling him to breathe. He wanted to shout that he *was* breathing, but did try to slow his heart down as he'd been ordered to. The room seemed to grow incredibly smaller as he looked around. And when it began to shift and roll, he put his head down. Something was very wrong.

"You've had a bit of a delay it seems. Just sit there and drink this." He felt something shoved into his hands. "And drink it quickly so I can refill it."

The tea tasted so delicious that he didn't mind draining the glass. As soon as he pulled it from his lips, another was pressed into his hands. He was drinking his third glass when he realized that he could raise his head without being sick. He looked at Ama, who was holding his hand.

"What was that? And what did you mean by a delay? Delay of what?" Jacob looked at Ama before he looked back at him. He was afraid of the answer and was about to tell him never mind, he didn't want to know when Ama spoke.

"You've just become like me. It was quicker than when I changed to faerie, but it's done now. Are you okay?" He nodded, still not sure what she was talking about. "I can hear your thoughts. Take a deep breath and then blow it out slowly."

He did as she said. Looking around the room, he realized that there was a pattern that he'd not seen before and said so. Jacob laughed a little, then stood up. He helped Sebastian up as well.

"You're going to be just fine. And yes, there is a pattern. You can read it now, correct?" Sebastian looked around the room again and then at where he supposed the starting point was. "There you have it. Now tell me what it says."

"Amarizi and Sebastian Bowen, you are hereby requested to come to the Ball of Faeries on October twelfth at midnight." He watched the room shift again and more letters appeared. "You may bring your families, but you must also bring the book. Sincerely, the High Council."

He looked at Ama and then at Jacob, who was grinning like he'd just won the lottery. Sebastian was beginning to dislike this wizard a great deal. When he stepped toward the door, Sebastian called him back.

"I don't know what's going on here. You said that I've changed. Okay, I get that, but who is the High Council, and why do we have to go to this ball? And just what book are they talking about? There isn't even an address for us to go to."

"You're taking this remarkably well for a man who only days ago didn't know a thing about faeries." Jacob nodded to the boxes just behind them. "Have a seat and I'll tell you what I can. The rest? Well, I'm not sure who will tell you that."

"The rest?" Ama looked at him when Jacob nodded at her question. "I thought you'd told me everything when you met up with me all those years ago. And now you tell me there's more? And the first words out of your mouth had better be to tell me why you keep bowing before us and call us lord and lady all of the sudden."

"It's the title given to mated couples such as you." Jacob raised his hand when Sebastian started to speak. "I'm not able to tell you all because it is forbidden for me to tell you. There will be another that will meet you at the ball. And when you meet him, he will be able to tell you everything."

Sebastian nodded and pulled Ama closer to him. "You said you can tell us some. How much? And will not knowing the rest get her hurt if that prick comes to get her?"

"No. Nothing will harm her between now and then." Sebastian found the wording of that statement odd, but before he could question it, Jacob spoke again. "You're to protect each other, now and forever. Your ability to adapt so well, my lord, is going to serve you well. But in the coming days, you'll begin to feel the effects of her power on you. You'll need to make sure that you drink as much as you can. And drink lots of juice if you can. I know that it is difficult at times, but fresh-squeezed is much better. Also, when you start to get more control over your mind, you may want to establish a link to your family, both of you. It will help you later, I think."

"I have a link with my family." Jacob shook his head at him. "What do you mean no? I've been able to contact them all my life."

"But you're no longer just a panther." Jacob touched his wrist and he felt the connection. "You'll need to be a panther when you first contact them. Khan will need you to contact him sooner rather than later. I can feel his frustration at not being able to contact you. If you'd like, my lord, I can tell him that you're having difficulties. But you're all right?"

Sebastian nodded, feeling a great deal like *Alice in Wonderland.* He was the rabbit running down the holes, and he was constantly running one step behind. He looked at

Ama, who was staring at him strangely. He asked her what was going on.

"Your marks are showing up like mine. Not as fancy, but I can see them." She reached for her purse and dug something out and handed it to him. "Look into this mirror and you can see it."

He *was* marked like her, just not as fancy or as much like she'd said, but he had a feeling that it might change at any minute. He handed her back the mirror, not wanting to think about that right now. Jacob nodded to Ama, and she tightened her grip on Sebastian's hand.

"You need to shift, my lady, before too much longer. You'll need to be fully faerie when you go to the ball, and you will need to have some control." He looked at him. "You, as well, my lord. The council will expect you both to be able to spread your wings when they ask you to."

"Wings?" He felt the walls begin to shift again and lowered his head and closed his eyes. "You said shift. I'm assuming you don't mean me to shift to a panther."

"No, my lord, you'll need to be able to be faerie when they ask. It will make things go so much smoother." Like he gave a shit right now, but didn't tell Jacob. "Sire, you're doing it again."

"Jacob, I like you. I really do, but I need for you to shut the fuck up right now." Ama giggled and he thought he heard Jacob chuckle. "This room? Was this done this way to bring us down here so they could invite us to this ball thing?"

"Yes. It will be put back to order before we leave here." Jacob sat down on one of the lower boxes. "The book is called the Book of Secrets. Your brother has a list of all beings, and you are to have a book that tells the secrets that his list doesn't cover. Like things that they have done that could get them brought before the courts, things that have been done to others as well. You have the book already. It is among the things that were brought to your home when Amarizi came to you. This book will never be read by anyone but you two."

"So we have a hit list of sorts." Jacob nodded. "Why do I have to take it to the ball if you said no one else can look at it?"

"You misunderstood. I said you will be the only two who can read it. And as the last earth faeries couple, you are the only ones who can read it. There are no more like you two."

Sebastian spoke up before Jacob could. "But we're going to a faerie ball. How is that possible if we're the only couple left? Unless there won't be anyone else there but us and this council. And if that's the case, why have a ball at all? Why don't they just come here, for instance? We can have a few drinks and get to know each other that way."

"It's a ball for you to meet your subjects." Ama looked at him, then they both turned to Jacob. "Yes, as I have said, you're the last of your kind. The king and queen of faeries."

"And our subjects would be what? Tinker Bell and some of the other little characters that I can't think of right now?" He looked at Jacob. "I know. I know, I'm projecting again. So what? You've just told us that we're a king and queen, and if that doesn't make a person project, I'm not sure what would."

"Sire, would it help you to know why you were chosen to be her king? It's a very good story and one you'll enjoy." Sebastian nodded. "Good. Many years ago you were playing in the field behind your home. You were seven and as curious as they come. And while sitting in this field you laid back and watched the other creatures, the tiny ones, move from flower to flower as they gathered food for their families. Then you saw her. Do you remember her?"

"No. No, that was a dream. I'd fallen asleep and dreamed about her." Jacob shook his head, and Sebastian closed his eyes as he told them what he'd seen. "She was sitting on a rock...no, a stone. She was little, about the size of my palm. And we sort of stared at each other for a long while. She stood up after a few minutes and when she did, I saw that she had wings. When she flew to my knee and sat down again, I asked her what her name was. But before she could answer me, the neighbor's cat came along."

"You protected her, it's told." Sebastian looked at Jacob as he continued the tale. "When the cat came near her, you started throwing rocks at it. When that didn't work, you scooped up the little brownie and put her into your pocket, telling her she'd be safe there. She was, too, and when you got rid of the cat, you set her on a tree stump gently, and she bowed before you then left."

"I thought she was a dream. I never told anyone that before." Jacob nodded. "How did you know?"

"She told me, and when I went to look for you, I knew that you'd be perfect for the new queen when she was old enough." Jacob said that he needed to leave and stood up. "You'll need to be ready for the ball. I would suggest that you practice your wings when you can."

As he moved through the room, all the destruction that had been in the room was put back to order. The writing on the walls and floor disappeared and everything else was set to rights. Sebastian looked at Ama.

"We need to see if we have that power."

Chapter 8

Wanera stood very still and watched Jacob the wizard leave the building. He'd been told that the wizard was in the human realm and had come to see it for himself. Wanera hated the man. As he moved out of the empty building, he had started to follow him when a couple came out behind him a few seconds later. He watched them as they got into the car and drove by his hiding place. He went into the building to see what they had been doing.

Their scent hit him as soon as he crossed the threshold. Earth faeries, both of them. Wanera staggered slightly and held onto the wall as he tried to absorb what he knew. The female had a mate. And the mate was a panther.

"Could this get any worse?" he cried out. "Can I have one fucking thing go right? Please, someone answer me."

Of course, since no one could see him, no one was going to answer him. He moved around the room, smelling everything they'd touched. Their scent to him was like a drug, pure and fresh. He wanted to hunt them down and lick them both. But he couldn't, not now. A mated pair of faeries was as sacred as anything he'd ever known, and she was no longer an option for him to breed with.

"Unless he dies or gives her to me." The second part was completely out of the question. He knew that panthers mated for life and that faeries went even beyond that. But if the male died suddenly, then Wanera could take her. A plan was forming even as he asked to be brought back to his realm.

"Get me all you can on the place I was just at. I want the name of the person who owns it and where they live." The being nodded. "Also, let me know of any panther family's around that area, how big they are, and who the leader is."

"Yes, sire." He watched as the being started pounding on the keys. "I have a name, my lord, but only a last. The name on the deed is Bowen and nothing more."

He nodded as the being continued to work. After about ten more minutes, the being turned to him. His face was bright with happiness, not something you saw much of around there.

"Bowen is the name of the family of panthers there as well. The leader's name is Khan and there is a large family of them. Six brothers, as well as a few members that are nearby who report to him and sometimes serve him. The parents of the family are still alive as well, and they live on a compound of sorts about seventeen miles from the building." Wanera smiled. "There is a rumor that a female has joined their ranks recently. There is not much said about her, but it is reputed that she is very beautiful. She is supposed to be mated to the brother called Sebastian. He owns and operates a shop of sorts. I don't have the details on that, but I do have an address."

"Yes. Good, it's all coming together. Send me to his place of business and make sure that I can be visible to the inhabitants of the place. I would also like to look like a business man. Can you do that?" The being nodded, and he was suddenly dressed in a suit. Not something he'd normally wear, but he did want to appear normal. Or as normal as humans could be.

He felt the air shift and he was suddenly standing outside another building. At least this time he was a little more prepared. He opened the door and stepped into a realm not like anything he'd ever seen.

Wanera knew what a computer was but not much more than that. He had purchased everything that the being had asked for, but beyond that, he knew nothing. There were so many things on the shelves and walls that he put his hands into his pockets, afraid that if he touched something, the entire thing would come down on him. The woman coming toward him looked chipper, something that he hated most in humans.

"Hi. What can I help you find today?" He looked around, wondering if he should have had an idea in mind, and saw the sign advertising hard drives.

"I need a new hard drive. I want to have one for my be...friend." She started nodding and he found himself being led to a shelf filled with boxes and computers. "He said that he needed two of them."

"Two?" He panicked, thinking he should just leave. "Oh, does he have a desktop and a laptop he needs to put them in?"

He nodded. "Yes, that's right. He does have one that sits on his desk. Laptop? Yes, I believe he has something that he puts there as well."

She nodded again and he felt safe. But he realized after several minutes that she was talking about something other than computers and was going on about her boyfriend. He looked around the store for someone to save him when a large man came out of the back office. It was the man from the building.

"Excuse me." Walking away from the woman had no apparent effect on her mouth moving. She continued as if he were still standing there.

He was nearly to the man when he realized two things at once. The man was a panther with a faerie mate, and the man knew what he was. Wanera backed up when he started toward him. Before he could call his being to be brought home, the large man had his hand around his throat.

"What are you doing here?"

Wanera struggled against his hold but couldn't break loose. That was the problem when he was in the human world trying to look like one of them. He was just like them when it came to his magic, too.

"I came to speak to you about your mate. I would like it if you were to give her to me." The man shook him hard, and Wanera felt his teeth snap together over his tongue. "She means more to me than she will to you. I'm going to be asked to step down if she doesn't come to me freely."

"Are you fucking insane? You don't honestly believe that I'd give up my mate to you simply because you asked, do you?" Wanera wanted to tell him that's exactly what he thought, but the man didn't give him a chance to answer. "You must be all kinds of stupid if you think that. Or you're joking with me. Is this supposed to be funny? If it is, I'm not finding the joke."

"I'm neither stupid nor joking with you. I am very serious. I will pay you handsomely for her." The man shook him again and then the room seemed to tighten. He looked up to see Jacob standing just behind the man who held him. Reaching to his being, he begged to be brought home immediately. In seconds he was gasping for breath on the floor with the being handing him some hot tea.

~~~

Sebastian paced in front of her. Ama could almost feel sorry for his brothers. Each of them had come in the door almost as soon as Sebastian had gotten home. Khan had been first and then the others had followed in pairs, the brothers and their mates if they had one. Reed came in last and sat down nearest the little boy George. Even his mom and dad sat on the couch watching their son.

"I think the man is insane. He would have to be, don't you think? To believe that I'd actually sell my mate to him means he's off his noodle, right?" He wasn't talking to any one person, and none of the people in the room answered. Ama thought they were afraid of him. "He came into my store and asked about hard drives, then came to me to talk about buying my mate."

"You should know that your eyes are glowing, Sebastian." She looked over at Dylan as he spoke to his brother. "Not to mention I can see the sigil coming out pretty good now, too."

Sebastian stopped moving for the first time in over twenty minutes. He stared around the room for a minute before he looked at her. She smiled at him and wondered again why she ever thought not having him as a mate was a good thing.

"I've been going through some changes of my own. I'm not sure how much you guys know about Ama, but she's an earth faerie. And because we're mated, I'm sort of one, too. Actually, I am one. She and I are the king and queen of faeries."

Walker stood up and put his hand on his forehead before he turned to the room. "I'm sorry to tell you guys this, but Sebastian has gone over the deep end. He has delusional grandeur. A serious disease that men with huge heads and egos get when they think they're king."

"Shut up, you ass, and sit down." Sebastian seemed to relax a little after that. "I am king to Ama's queen. We talked with Jacob the wizard today, and he told us."

Ama looked around the room, and the only people who didn't look shocked by his news were Dylan and his mate. Jonny winked at her and smiled. She knew that they'd spoken somehow.

"So, let me get this straight. You're a computer shop owner as well as a panther that just happens to be a king. Works for me." Caitlynne sat back and smiled. "You might want to have business cards made. It will save time in trying to get people to remember all your titles. They are titles, right? I mean, should we just call you Ding-Dong Panther and be done with it?"

He growled low at her and Ama started to laugh. When he turned to her and glared, she simply raised her brow at him and he flushed. She wondered what he would have done if she had laughed harder.

"Seriously though, we have to figure out what to do about this guy. I don't think he's going to quit now that he's figured out where you are. You said that he could take Ama from you if you're dead, right?" Sebastian nodded at his dad. "Then you think that's next on his agenda? You think he might try and kill you just to get her?"

"What does he want you for anyway?" Reed flushed. "Sorry, that didn't come out quite right. What I meant was, why you? I mean, yes, you're all that, but what about you makes him willing to come to this place and take you?"

"I'm a faerie, and I'm the only species other than his own that can get pregnant without him being my mate. Sort of like humans. If the time is right and he's there, then—" She stopped talking when Sebastian growled at her. "I didn't say it was right, you overbearing pig. I'm only saying it's true."

"But why is he so hyped up to get you now? I mean, you've been a faerie all your life. Why is he just now trying to get you to come to him and so in a hurry to get you now?" His mom looked around the room. "Does he have some sort of deadline he's trying to meet?"

"In a way." They all looked at Dylan as he continued. "His name is Wanera. He's an underlord in a different realm. He came here specifically to get Ama because of the reasons she said. And he has to have a child or someone to take over his realm by summer solstice. If not, he is put to death. There isn't a lot of use for his kind once they've served their time. If he has a child, he can stay on until such time that his child is old enough to rule the realm, then he can retire, not die."

"A child is all he wants from her?" They looked at George. "That's the stupidest thing I've ever heard. So he would just have a baby with her, then what? Toss her away? Who would love and nurture the child? Not him, that's for sure. He sounds like a real asshole."

"He's not very bright either. When he was in the store, he asked to buy a hard drive for two computers. Debby said that he acted like he was just buying something at random." Sebastian came and sat next to Ama while he continued. "I could smell him. That's the reason I came out of the office. I thought something was on fire. Then when I saw him…I could see him."

"See him?" She looked at him when he nodded. "You could see a demon lord in his true self? Wow, I've never done that before. Do you think he knew what you were?"

He shrugged. "I don't know. He knew I was your mate, but he didn't say anything about the rest. Do you suppose he thinks that we're just mates and nothing more?"

"That could work to your advantage if he came to you again. I mean, didn't you say that Jacob said you were like the all-powerful Oz or some crap?" Monica laughed as she continued. "Does that mean you have powers over him? Could you like, order him to be gone or something?"

"No." They looked at Jacob as he entered the room with a large tray. "I brought sandwiches. And some fresh juice. It is important that you drink more than you are, my lord."

He sat the tray down and each of them took a sandwich. Ama watched the others around the room as Jacob moved to each of them, giving them tea instead of the juice. When he sat down, he looked ready to tell them what they wanted…needed to know.

"Wanera is something different than most of the other underlords. He is a low man on the ladder of beings in his realm, but he is still powerful. And yes, he is somewhat stupid, and knows little about this realm at all…and that's a good thing. He has beings that work for him, hundreds of them, that pick up after him and even run most of the day-to-day work, but he does have magic."

"So how do we keep him from taking Ama from me?" Ama wanted to know that as well. "If he comes here again, how do I kill him? Because I get the feeling that's going to be the only way to stop him."

"He's afraid of you." Ama started to speak when Jacob raised his hand. "I'm sorry, my lady, but I just left the council. They've given permission for you to have a visitor. He…he isn't well, so please be careful of him. He is —"

"Right here, you idiot." The man that seemed to suddenly appear stood tall and seemingly very weak with something, possibly an illness. But as he walked toward her, she could see that he was hurt. He favored his left leg, and one arm seemed not to work as well as the other. He stood in front of her but spoke to Sebastian.

"I'd like your permission to hug your mate please, Lord Sebastian. But you should know that I'm going to do it anyway, so either get over it or give it to me." He smiled at her. "You're more beautiful than your mother."

"You knew her?" He nodded and cupped the back of her head and pulled her to him. "I don't understand, how did you...? You smell like her, like I remember her smelling."

"I would yes," he said, his voice full of emotion, so much that she looked up at him. "You're my daughter, Amarizi. My only child."

She felt Sebastian come near them and the man holding her stiffened. "I won't...we were told that you were dead. And coming from a man that said he couldn't lie to us, we believed him."

Ama pulled back and looked up at him. There was nothing at all in her memories to make her believe what he said was true, yet she believed him. Helping him to the chair next to the couch, she watched him try and get comfortable. She realized then that it wasn't just the injuries that made him uncomfortable, but the people in the room. She introduced them to him.

"I'm Lord Fryda, faerie. I've been...damn it all the hell; I thought this would be easier. Why did you think that I'd be welcome here?" He glared at Jacob. "I think it's time I went back to—"

"Oh, hush up and sit still." Corrine handed him a pillow. "Put that under your thigh and be quiet for a minute. Reed, go and get the heating pad out of the bathroom and bring it back to him. George, give him that footstool. He won't ask for it. I can see where your daughter gets her stubbornness."

"Madam, do you know that I can turn you into a pixie with the flick of my finger?" He shoved the pillow under his thigh when she pointed at it. "I'm a powerful faerie and a man of my own rights. I'm not accustomed to being treated as a child."

"Then stop acting like one and I'll think about not treating you like one. Maybe you are a powerful faerie, but right now you're on my turf, and I say you'll hush up." Corrine looked at Ama. "No wonder it took you so long to agree to be Sebastian's mate. If this is the gene pool you're coming from, it's a small wonder he ever got close to you."

Reed came back with the heating pad, and Corrine plugged it in and put it on Fryda's arm. Ama could see the shocked look on his face when it started to warm the area that hurt. Her dad mumbled a thank you and Corrine nodded and sat down. He looked around the room.

"You're all good people. We—the other beings and I— have heard great things about you. The facts that you've taken on so much and have helped so many of us notwithstanding, you're also polite, most of the time, and you have good heads on your shoulders." He laughed a little. "I suppose you want to know why I'm not dead. Well, you can thank Jacob over there. When he found me after Wanera tried to kill me, laying there near death I was. He protected me while the earth healed me. Took it a long time, too."

"You didn't want to live." Ama let the words slip out before she could stop them. "I'm sorry, but you seem so bitter about him saving you that I thought that…"

"You're right. I didn't want to live. But he made me. Said you'd need me someday, and I guess he was right. And if you knew Jacob as well as I do, then you'd know that him turning himself into a panther was a great honor for me. He doesn't care for shifting." He looked at Sebastian, who was still standing so close to her. "You think you've got something to say? Then do it. I'm too old and too beat up to have you standing over me like some sort of protector. I can take care of myself."

"You didn't heal because you gave her all your powers." Her dad looked up at Sebastian sharply. "You were dying and you sent her everything. You were thinking you'd just die so she'd be safe. That's why you haven't healed yet. You don't have enough left in you to do so."

Jacob laughed. "I told you he was sharp. Yes, my lord, you're correct. He's a stubborn bastard—pardon my language—that won't let anyone help him. So he suffers. And we all have to hear about it. Daily. Almost hourly."

"Now see here. I saved her, didn't I? He couldn't take her from her mother, could he?" Her dad looked at her. "I had to make sure you and her were fine. I couldn't fail the two of you again."

"But she wasn't fine, was she? She died a broken-hearted woman because you left her." Ama stood up. "I'm not sure how I feel about you coming into my life after all this time. The people in this room have been far kinder to me than any other person has been in my whole life. You left us when healing. You could have kept my mother alive and well until she died. Well, I don't really care for you, or for that matter, know why you've come here."

She turned to Sebastian and took his hand. Her father sat there for several minutes before he spoke. She had hoped that he'd just leave, but apparently he thought he had something more to say.

"I know what a broken heart feels like. I feel it daily. Not just because I couldn't see you grow up, but because I couldn't protect you or your mom when Wanera showed up. He beat me because I was a fool, a fool who thought he could win against a being like him. And because of that, I lost everything." He stood up. "I'm sorry that I left you. I'm even sorrier that your mom died and never told you about anything that you were. She…she was my own true love."

"So now you plan to leave her again?" They looked at Jack. "What a crock of shit. Sit down, you cranky prick. We have a situation on our hands and you're going to help us fix it. If you want to leave afterwards, then more power to you. But for now your ass is going to help us. Oh, and for the record, you are a whiner and I, for one, can't stand whiners. So either grow some balls or shut the fuck up."

Ama's dad turned to Jack. He looked ready to do major damage to her sister-in-law, but when Ama went to stand in front of her to protect Jack, her dad raised his hand.

"You're a pain in the ass. Has anyone ever told you that before?" Jack told him plenty. "I would imagine so. I'm staying, but not because of you. I'm staying because I need to."

"Whatever floats your boat, old man." Jack moved forward and put out her hand. "We're not going to have any problems are we, you and I?"

"Probably," he told her. "But I'm sure you can take it."

And just like that, he was accepted into the clan. Ama looked at Sebastian, who was trying his best not to laugh. Soon he couldn't help it, but it mattered little. The entire room was laughing.

"All right, tell us what you know about Wanera the demon." Khan started taking notes as her dad spoke. It was going to be a long night.

Chapter 9

Sebastian watched the last car pull out of the driveway. Fryda had left a little while ago with Jacob. The two of them were still arguing as they faded from the room. Sebastian had a feeling that the two of them had been at it for a great many years, even before Fryda had been hurt. He started up the steps to his home when he saw Ama standing on the deck. He went to her.

"You know that he's not going to play by any rules, don't you?" He nodded as he pulled her back against his chest. "Jacob seems to think he's going to try something stupid, like simply taking me without permission."

"He more than likely will try. But he's got a surprise coming for him if he does that. I'm not going to let him hurt you." She nodded. He looked out to the trees in their backyard and nuzzled her neck. He wanted her out there and wondered how he could take her when she wasn't a panther.

"I can shift." He stilled. "I couldn't before we bonded, but I know I can now. Would you like to go for a run?"

He had to clear his throat twice before he could speak. "How do you know you can shift? Did you try it already?"

She put out her arm and he watched it begin to morph and fur, fine at first then fuller, began to grow along her skin.

She stretched out her hand and he could see it changing into a paw, large dark nails beginning to protrude from the fur.

"I thought about it earlier when I was in the bathroom and it happened. I can do other things, too." Her hands shifted again and he saw her skin change from fur to feathers. Initially dark as the fur, they changed to lighter colors until they resembled those of a barn owl.

"Baby, shift into a panther for me. I want to watch you." She pulled away from him, and he watched her unbutton her blouse and drop it to the deck. Then her bra. His breath caught when the moon came from behind a cloud and seemed to shine on the silkiness of her breasts. When she bent to take off her pants, he had to grab the railing. Her ass looked good enough for him to eat. She turned and looked at him from her bent position.

"You're staring at my bottom." He nodded. "Well stop it. It's very strange to know you're looking at me like...you look hungry."

"I am, and if you don't hurry, that run we were going to take is going to be delayed." She wiggled her ass at him and, while still bent over, tore her panties from her body. "Christ, you're lovely."

Going up behind her, he unsnapped his pants. He had to be inside of her now rather than later. When she moaned, he fisted his cock and told her to hold onto the railing. She moved to it and braced her hands on it. He moved again, this time close enough that he could rub his cock in her juices as they leaked from her.

"You're so wet. Christ, you're soaking wet." He slid his cock into her and pulled her hips back to him. "Baby, I'm not going to last if you keep this up."

She was rolling her hips up and down, and he could feel her tighten around his cock. Sebastian thought about her cat and how much he wanted to take her. He leaned over her, moving in and out of her slowly.

"I need you to shift for me. I'm going to let you go. Then I want you to shift and take off toward the woods." He nipped at her shoulder, drawing a little blood. "Then I'm going to come after you and take you to the ground and fuck your cat hard. My cat wants to mark you with his teeth and drink from you."

"Please. I need to come first. Help me to come." He slid his fingers over her curls, not touching her clit. "Sebastian, please, I ache."

He pulled from her body and she snarled at him. He nearly took her then, but the thought of fucking her in the woods as they were meant to made him take another step back.

"Shift, Amarizi, shift and run with me." Her body shivered as he watched. Then she leaned back on her heel as her body stretched tightly. When she began to change, he nearly forgot to breathe. He'd never seen anything so beautiful in his life. As soon as she was panther she took off, leaping over the railing like it was nothing more than a pebble.

He didn't even bother taking off his clothes before shifting, instead letting them tear off him, which fueled his already high state of arousal. He leapt the railing, too, landing a few feet from where she had, and took off. Her scent was calling him, and he was going to answer her.

He followed her for several minutes. Every time he got close, he would watch her take off again and let her. He loved the chase, and she seemed to like that he was chasing her. When he saw her move just in front of him, he jumped up and took her to the ground. His body covered her completely.

"I'm going to bite you harder this way. Are you all right with that?" She snarled at him and tried to bite him. *"You're only making this harder on yourself."*

"Fuck me, please, I beg of you. I can no longer stand this." He moved over her, and when her tail moved for him, he slammed home. *"Yes."*

Her scream of approval nearly had him coming. He leaned his body over hers, much like he had at the deck, only this time he used his heavy paws to hold her there. When she tried to fight him, he sank his teeth into her shoulder. It only seemed to make her fight more. He bit her harder until she finally stilled.

"You're going to pay for this." He let his cat have her as he spoke, his own mind moving away from the cat to let him have his way. *"Come for me, Amarizi, please come for me."*

He'd heard all his life that cat sex, especially when the male was as large as he was, held very little pleasure for the female. He had a feeling that Ama would enjoy this more than him. When she started to moan in his mind, he felt his cat bite her harder. As soon as she snarled at him again, his cat threw back his head and roared out his release. Ama was so tight around him that he knew she had come, too. Now he wanted her.

When his cat pulled away, sated, Sebastian shifted. His cock was throbbing with need and Ama turned and looked at him through her beautiful green cat eyes. He watched her body come back to itself, and before he could tell her that he needed her, she wrapped her hand around his cock.

"I want to taste you. I want to feel your cock in my mouth when you come." He nodded and stood up. "Will you come down my throat, Sebastian?"

"Yes. Christ, yes. Suck me, Ama. Wrap your mouth around me and—holy shit." He felt his eyes roll to the back of his head as she swallowed him. The tightness of her throat and the swallowing motion was nearly too much, but when he reached down to pull her head from him, he curled his fingers into her hair and held her there. All thought left his head as she brought him closer and closer to the edge, only to pull back and start again.

"Ama, finish me or let me fuck you. You're going to kill me." Her hands cupped his balls and he moaned her name. "Ama, I'm begging you."

She let him go with a little pop and he wanted to pounce on her. When she licked him again, he tightened his grip in her hair and watched her, his shallow breathing making him dizzy.

"Come like this. Then you can fuck me." She licked him from root to tip. "I want you to come all over me while you jerk off. I need to feel your hot cum on me."

He wrapped his free hand around his cock and began moving up and down its length. She never stopped licking him, so the ride was smooth. As soon as she nipped at him and gave his balls a gentle tug, he felt his climax rush up his cock from his feet and shoot forward.

Stream after stream shot from him as he watched her gather it on her tongue and swallow it down. Nothing had ever felt so right, so amazing. Sebastian saw her rub it onto her nipples as she squeezed her breasts and tweaked them. He held her head, not because he needed to hold her in place, but because he was going to fall if he didn't. He stood over her as his cock emptied and tried to catch his breath. But she wasn't finished with him and laid back on the grass.

"Take me. Fuck me hard and make me scream." He dropped to his knees and opened her bent legs. She was swollen, her clit hard and red. "Please, Sebastian, I need you."

He wanted to taste her like this, suckle her into his mouth and taste her cum, but he needed to be buried in her and dropped over her before he could change his mind. He didn't just slide into her but punched deep. Her cry made him still above her.

"More. I need...if you stop now, I'm going to kill you. Please." Leaning up so that he could take her as hard as he could, he used his entire body to fuck her, hard, fast strokes that made his muscles scream as he pounded into her. When she pulled him to her, her mouth over his chest, he felt her bite his hard muscle and scream against him. He licked her throat to her shoulder, and as he came with her he sank his teeth into her and tore at her flesh. This would leave a mark that everyone would see.

He dropped onto her and started to roll to his back so his weight wouldn't be too much when she stopped him by wrapping her legs around him. He looked down at her and saw tears in her eyes, and he cradled her in his arms.

"I'm so sorry, baby. I was really rough and I hurt you." She shook her head and he looked down at her again. "I didn't hurt you?"

"No, I loved it. I love you." He watched her for several seconds. Then she laughed. "Well? Don't you have something to say to me?"

"I love you as well. Yes, I do love you." He kissed her then, a slow and thorough kiss before lifting his head. "I love you so very much."

~~~

Wanera sat in the darkness of his lair and watched the flames of the fire dance around. He hurt in places he'd never hurt before, and he was sure that if he would look he'd see that he was injured in some way that was never going to heal. Shifting in his chair, he wondered if the man who had dared touch him was hurting like he was. He certainly hoped so. The knock at his door made him cringe, and when it opened, he glared at the being standing there.

"You've a visitor. She said that you called her." He nodded, glad now that he'd had the being call his healer. He stood up when she told him to.

"What have you been into? You smell of...." She leaned in and sniffed him. "You reek of humans. Have you been topside?"

"I have to see to a breeder. But one of them attacked me. Can you see what he's done to me, please?"

She snorted but told him to take off his shirt. He did as she said and stood before her in just his trousers. She walked around him three times before she touched him. When she put her hands on his shoulders, then to his neck, he winced from the pain.

"You've been more than touched. I think whoever it was drew blood." She looked closer and then looked up at him. "You've been touched by a powerful faerie and he drew your blood. You know what that means, don't you?"

He shook his head, but she was already pulling her coat back on. "Wait, what does that mean? He drew my blood. So what does that mean?"

"He must have some of it on him, right?" Wanera supposed that could be true and nodded. "Then he can come here and avenge whatever you did to him to make him hurt you. You're so fucked."

She was gone before he could ask her how to treat the rest of his pains. The faerie had his blood and now.... He stood up and went to find his being. The one from earlier was on break, he'd been told, so he had the one sitting at the computer look it up.

"I want to know if a faerie can come to this realm without my permission." The being shook his head. "Under no circumstances can he come here unless I say he can?"

"No, sire, no one can enter or leave this realm without your permission. They would have to be a fool to come here anyway with you being in charge. No, you are correct." Wanera turned to leave when the being spoke again. "Unless he has your blood. Then he can come and go as he pleases."

Wanera turned slowly and looked at the being sitting there with the stupidest expression on his face. He wanted to walk over and burn it off him. He was just getting ready to when he saw something on the screen.

"What was that?" He moved toward the screen that they forever seemed to be watching. "That bright blip, what is that?"

"I do not know, my lord. I was told to call to Bill when it appeared. Shall I do that now?" Wanera had no idea who "Bill" was until he appeared in the room. It was the being that helped him the most. He hadn't realized that they had names. He just thought they all called each other "being" as he did.

"That is the girl, sire. She is moving again. I have been watching her since you first asked me to. I must say, my lord, that she has gotten considerably brighter in the last several days."

"She's mated." The being nodded and moved to the seat now vacated by the other...he wondered what his name was and realized he really didn't care. "I think he's a panther and now he has some of my blood."

The being Bill turned to look at him. "Mayhap, my lord, he does not know he has it. And if he doesn't then perhaps he doesn't know what it will give him. He may be very stupid, sire."

He doubted that but said nothing, He stared, and the blip didn't move again. He asked Bill why not. He turned back to the keyboard and punched in a few more keys or whatever he had to do, and an address popped up.

"She works there. It is a pizza shop that a werebear owns and operates. Have you had one of them? Pizza, not bear, my lord." Wanera's mouth snapped closed on the story he was about to tell about a she-bear that he'd had once. She had been very chewy and he hadn't cared for the aftertaste. Then he realized what Bill had said.

"She has a job? What does she need to work for? If she belonged to me, I would never have her work." He glared at the screen. "Where does her mate go when she is slaving for him?"

"He, too, is at work." The screen moved at a dizzying speed and stopped when another blip appeared. "He is at his computer store. What I wouldn't give to go there and see the things he has."

Wanera looked at Bill. He'd been there, and found nothing extraordinary that would have made his voice sound like Bill's did when he talked about the things that might be in the store. Wanera looked at the equipment that he was using.

He'd noticed that the computers in the store were much smaller than this one. The screen here was thick and small, and it wasn't in color. The ones in the store had been in colors so bright that he'd been surprised by them, and at how thin the screens were. He also noticed that the keyboard that Bill used had letters missing; not keys gone, but the letters were no longer visible on them. He decided to have him a new computer set up soon, and tried to think what had been on the shelves. He gave up; there were just too many things he had no idea about.

"What if I took you there...to his store? Would you be able to purchase a more updated model that I could see in color on? This one is very primitive, and it's hard on my eyes." Bill turned to look at him, shock on his face. "You'd have to be invisible, as would I, but if you show me what you need, perhaps we can get it at another store."

"I could do that." He sounded so excited that Wanera was embarrassed. "I would be able to get the best for you, sire, if you so desired."

"Yes, the best would be good. Do you know what you need?" Bill nodded, reached into the top box sitting next to him, and handed him a file. "You'll have to come with me. I can't figure out any of that crap."

Seconds later, they were both standing next to the line of computers. They found everything they needed, and some things they didn't, within an hour. Next, they went to another store and found the same items, but their prices seemed a bit higher. Appearing in the store, Wanera was ignored for the better part of an hour before someone came to help him. Two hours later and a good deal broker, Wanera willed all the things home to the room where Bill was.

"Oh my, sire. You've gotten a filing cabinet as well?" He touched each item as he set it up. "And a video player, too?"

"It was free." It hadn't been, but when the man said that it was a must-have for a new computer, Wanera had seen no reason not to get it as well. "You'll have this set up when? I'd like to be able to watch without having to strain my eyes."

"Tomorrow when you rise, sire. I will have it set up for your pleasure." Wanera nodded and left him to it. He'd never given anyone anything before and had been...well, he'd been embarrassed. Going to his room, he decided that he needed a few things for in there, too, and made plans to visit a few of the other realms' homes to see what they had in the way of furniture. Going to his bed, Wanera felt good, but not great.

Maybe, he thought, if he did a good job at making his lair look good, his bride would be happy. He had a feeling that a happy mate would be a good deal easier to live with. He just didn't want any trouble right now or when the baby came along.

Closing his eyes, he tried to think if he'd ever seen a baby before. He didn't think so. If he had it had been so long that he could no longer remember. He began to think that having a mate long enough to breed with, then tossing her away, wasn't such a good plan. He might need her to help him with the child. He thought he'd heard somewhere that mates, female ones, were supposed to be good with children. Wanera fell asleep smiling.

Chapter 10

"Mistress, I was wondering if I may have a word with you." She turned to see Peter standing in the doorway to the kitchen. He looked like he was very nervous about something. She shoved the next load of dishes into the washer and turned and smiled at him.

"What is it? Have I done something to upset you?" He shook his head then frowned at her. "Come on, Peter, it can't be that bad."

"Mistress, I was wondering if you could...I would never ask if I...you see, there is...." He sat down at the table he often had lunch with her at. "I wish for my wife to have a child. I was wondering if you could see her."

She sat down beside him and tried to think. She had no idea what he was talking about and took a deep breath to try and figure this out. But he started talking again.

"I know that faeries have some powers. And you being an earth faerie would be a great deal more than the normal...I'm not saying this right. Let me begin from the start. My wife is pregnant. It's the tenth time we have tried."

She sat back, sad for them both. "What is it you think I can do? I mean, I don't know a great deal about my kind, but I'll help you in any way I can."

"You can heal the sick. I know this; I've read it in the tomes we have. But it is said that you can help a child, too, before it's born. I fear that if we lose this one, my wife will go as well. I can't lose her. I love her too much." He took her hand. "You need only to touch her and tell the child to hang on. And it will for you, my lady. I know it."

She nodded, and he pulled her out of the chair and toward the dining area, a place she'd never been since she'd started working there. But there was no one in the big room except a small woman who sat in a booth. Peter took Ama over and sat beside the small woman.

"My lady Ama, this is my mate and the love of my life, Doris. Doris, this is my dishwasher, Amarizi Bowen." The woman nodded and stood up.

"My lady." Doris bowed. "He never said that you were...of course, he couldn't tell me, but you're a queen, aren't you?"

"So they tell me." Ama looked at her swollen belly. "You're not just a little pregnant, are you?"

"Seven months. But the doctor says that I may lose this one as well. He said that I have a problem holding them safely. Bed rest doesn't work, but I want this one so badly." Peter held her as she cried. Ama wanted to go and find the doctor who would say something like that to a woman and expect her to be happy about it. Ama reached for Monica and asked her if she knew of a good doctor. The two of them had been talking about some of her panther-related questions.

"I have a very good doctor, and he just happens to be nearby. We both are. Khan and I were having lunch with Walker and Caitlynne before they went back to DC to finish up things there. Can we come to you? And Walker wants to know the name of the doctor she's using now."

Ama asked the couple and then repeated the information to Monica. She said she'd be there in ten minutes, to have Doris sit down and put her feet up. When she arrived fifteen minutes later, she had not only Walker, but Caitlynne and Khan with her. They each had a bag in their hands.

"I've brought help. And you need to find another doctor. Yours is a quack." Walker took Doris's blood pressure and temperature. "You're as healthy as a bear, aren't you?"

Monica sat back but said little. Ama knew she was watching the pregnant woman until Walker turned to look at them both. He didn't look happy, and his next words confirmed it.

"There was a rumor going around before I left the hospital that Dr. Anderson was poisoning his patients. Not to kill them but to give them a miscarriage. I tried to figure out more, but he moved out of the hospital setting a few weeks later and I thought he'd retired. Apparently not." Walker sat down and looked at Doris. "You've been given a vitamin, correct?"

"Yes." Doris reached into her purse and handed him the bottle. Walker opened it and sniffed it. "He told me to take them twice a day. Should I take more?"

"No. They're toxic. And as they build up in your system, they slowly kill your unborn child. You've known that, haven't you?"

Doris flushed. "I haven't been taking them for a few months. And tomorrow...I think he knew it, and he was telling me that I need a transfusion. It was set up for me to go in tomorrow so he could pump me up full of those things. I decided...I told Peter that I'd rather die than to go do it, and he brought me here."

"He more than likely just saved your life and your children's." Walker looked at Caitlynne. "And my lovely wife

125

here would like to do everything in her power to make sure it doesn't happen again."

"I'd like to have you come to the clinic we're opening in a few weeks." Doris nodded at Khan and Ama raised a brow. "I don't tell everyone everything I'm doing. Monica and I have been thinking about it for some time and I talked to Walker about it yesterday. With the president retiring, he's going to have a bit more time on his hands now and has agreed to help us."

"And I would very much like it if you came to work for us." Doris flushed again at Monica's invitation. "You're a secretary, aren't you? We're going to need someone to help out in the office."

"I'd like that. I haven't been...my boss told me that I couldn't come back after this baby was born. He said that his own wife needed to get out of the house more and she wanted my job. We were...Peter and I were wondering how we were going to make it." She smiled. "I don't think he'll be so happy to have her there when he finds out she can't file a thing and thinks answering the phone is beneath her."

They all laughed. And when Doris stood to leave, she hugged Ama tightly. "Thank you, my lady. I can see why Peter thinks so highly of you."

"He is a wonderful man, and you two are going to be great parents. I know it." After another hug from her, Peter simply nodded. She figured he'd know about the male touching thing more than anyone.

Ama went back to the kitchen to finish the dishes when she heard a chair scrape across the floor. She turned to see Monica sitting there smiling at her.

"Peter is making us dinner. I've called Sebastian and the others, and they're coming over as well." She nodded. "I have a favor to ask you."

"Anything." Monica smiled and patted the seat next to her. "You're not going to ask me to leave Sebastian, are you? If you do, I'm going to have to tell you no."

Monica laughed. "No. Nothing like that. I need your job. Not me precisely, but someone I know. You see, there is this man who works for us. He's the gardener...I think you met him."

"Yes, Conrad I think his name is." Monica nodded. "What does that have to do with my job here?"

"His son. He had a son that's been in a bit of trouble with the law. Stealing and vandalism just to name a few. I've been talking with the judge, and he said that he'd release him to work if I found someone that would keep him in line."

"And Peter agreed." Monica shook her head. "Then I don't understand. If you don't want him to work for Peter then.... You are asking me first."

"Yes. It would only be fair. I didn't know if you'd agree or not, and didn't want Peter to think you're keeping this job because you feel you owe him. You don't, you know. We do, but you don't."

"How so? I needed a job when no one else would hire me. He didn't really want to hire me because he knew what I was, but he did. He's a wonderful man."

Monica smiled as she stood up. "And he kept you here for Sebastian. If he hadn't hired you, where would you be right now?"

She didn't know and thought Monica knew it. She looked around the room that she had come to like because it gave her a sense of pride to have a job. She looked back at Monica.

"If Peter agrees, I can let the boy have the job. But if he screws up one thing, I'm coming after his ass." Monica told her she'd not have it any other way.

~~~

Khan watched Sebastian and Ama and wondered not for the first time in the past few days what was going to happen to them once this thing with the demon was over. Would they be required to go to some other place to be in some castle, or would they be able to live here and work? He wanted them here. He wanted them all here. He looked at Walker when he sat down next to him, taking his last slice of pizza.

"George isn't going to be happy with his favorite uncle when I don't bring him home leftovers." George was Walker's little boy, and he and Khan had a blast together when he came to visit his cousins. "I'm going to tell him his dad had his piece."

"I already talked to Peter. He's making me one to take him. He'll think his dad is the greatest." Khan was pretty sure the kid already did. "Your daughter is going to break hearts when she grows up, don't you think?"

"She'll never date, so it's a moot point. I'm training her how to unman the first person who tries anything with her, too." Walker laughed, and they were joined by Sebastian. "You gonna get your pretty mate married to you before you have a baby?"

He reached into his pocket and pulled out the little box and handed it to Khan. Opening it under the table so no one could see, he whistled. It was the biggest emerald he'd ever seen.

"It matches her eyes." Khan nodded at his brother as he handed it back. "I was going to ask her tonight, but Monica called and asked me to come here. I guess I'll have to wait now."

"Why?" Sebastian flushed. "You don't think she's going to turn you down, do you? Christ, the woman can't take her eyes off you. She loves you too much for that to happen."

"I'd do it now. What better place for her to turn you down than in front of family and friends. It will be something I laugh about for decades." Walker slapped Sebastian on the shoulder. "Go for it. She's not going to turn you down."

Sebastian stood up and started toward Ama. Khan held his breath, thinking he was going to chicken out, when he suddenly dropped to his knee. The room grew quiet as they all turned to them. Khan felt Monica move up behind him and put her hand on his shoulder. He was as happy as he'd ever been.

"Amarizi Auburn, I love you with all my heart, and was wondering if you'd do me the honor of marrying me. And just so you know, Walker thinks you're going to turn me down." She looked at Walker and stuck her tongue out.

"Give her the ring, moron." Khan laughed when Sebastian nearly fell over trying to get it out of his pocket. He'd never seen his brother so flustered before.

He handed her the box and then took it back. He started to hand it to her again when he looked at Khan. "Take it out and put it on her finger. Christ, are you this stupid in bed, too?"

"No, he is not." Ama turned bright red when she realized what she'd said. "Behave, Khan, or I'll turn you into a frog."

"Amarizi Auburn, will you please marry me? I promise for as long as we live I will try to make you as happy as I am right now. I'll keep the toilet seat down and I'll even make the bed every day if you say yes."

"Yes, I'll marry you." He stood up and pulled her into his arms and swung her around the room. Khan couldn't believe how relieved he was that she'd said yes.

Khan pulled Monica to him and kissed her hard on the mouth. "What was that for? If you think this is going to get you lucky later, you might be right."

"I'm lucky right now. As lucky as any man, human or otherwise, has ever been." He pulled her down to nibble on her ear as he whispered against it. "You're in heat again."

When she looked at him, he could see her desire flare to life. Christ, he wanted her right now. Taking her hand to his mouth, he licked along the vein that heated under his touch. She moaned softly, and he nipped at her flesh.

"How much longer do we have to be here?" He stood up and started for the door. "Hurry, Khan, please?"

If anyone spoke to them as they were leaving, he didn't hear. He needed his wife right now and there was going to be hell to pay if someone tried to stop him. When he got her to the car, he knew that he wasn't going to make it, and pressed her against the trunk and held her there.

"I need you right now." She nodded and rolled over to her belly with her legs spread. Reaching under her tiny skirt, he tore her panties off as he ripped his zipper open. Tiny teeth hit the pavement. Before he could think about where they were, he slammed into her heat.

"Fuck, you're so tight." He pressed her down on the lid and ripped her shirt off her shoulder. "I need you to come when you can because the way I feel right now, I won't be able to wait for you."

He slammed into her hard, and each time she pressed back against him. Grabbing a handful of her hair, he pulled her up so he could lick along her shoulder. She tasted like heat, her body ready to receive his. As soon as his balls began to fill and tighten, he reached to her clit and pinched hard. She screamed and bit his arm that he held her with. His canines burned for her; his cat snarled as he bit her. Her hot-spiced blood filled his mouth at the same time he roared out his release.

Panting, he held her. She lay across the lid of the trunk and smiled at him. He kissed her where he'd bitten her and licked the wound closed. Her heavy sigh made him nuzzle her neck.

"You're a very impatient man. We might have made this last a little longer if you'd gotten me to the bed first." He chuckled, knowing that she'd needed him as badly as he had her. "Next time you know I'm in heat, you should let me know in a less public place. I know everyone in that room knew where we were going."

"I'm sure they did." He kissed her shoulder, then stood up. He looked down at his ruined pants. "You're very hard on my clothing, my lady. I should just learn to wear jogging pants everywhere we go."

"Why do you think I wear skirts now? I swear the last time I wore a pair of jeans out, you tore them off me so badly that I had to go home nearly naked." He smiled at that memory. He'd feasted on her twice before they got home. She slapped him on the arm.

"What? I was thinking about how poorly I treat you." She snorted and moved away from him. "Monica, I want you again. But if you want to wait, I can take us closer to home."

She laughed and got into the car. He moved to the driver's side, both sad and happy that they'd driven themselves. Had they come in the limo, he could have had her again in the back seat. Oh well, he'd just have to find a place for them to play on the way home.

"Do you think they'll be all right, Khan? Ama and Sebastian, do you think that this demon will be defeated by them?" He nodded. "I hope so. But I can't help but wonder what's going to happen to them after. Do you think that they'll have to go somewhere to rule or something?"

"I was thinking the same thing tonight. I hope not. Walker and Caitlynne will be coming home for good soon, and I'd hate to lose another brother so soon after that. I want them all around us." She nodded but looked sad. "You like her, don't you?"

"I do. She's very brilliant. So are the others. Caitlynne is amazing, and her plan to take care of Anderson in the morning is great. Jack is such a mouthy woman, but there is something about her that makes you want to smack her one minute and hug her the next. And Jonny? She's just simply amazing. I love her and her wit so much."

He waited for her to say more, and when she didn't, he glanced over at her. "What is it, Monica? You're very sad all of the sudden."

"She's very special. I don't mean the faerie part, just herself. Sebastian loves her very much." He nodded, waiting. "I wonder if he knows just how lucky he is."

Khan was pretty sure he knew. The man was besotted with his mate. Taking Monica's hand in his, he kissed it. When she smiled at him, he felt like the king of the world and told her so.

"You're just trying to butter me up so you can tie me to the bed again. Well, I got news for you. It's my turn, and I'm looking forward to strapping you down and taking my time tasting every inch of you."

He nearly drove them off the road. He looked over at her, hoping she wasn't kidding when she winked at him. He pressed a little harder on the gas pedal, no longer looking for a nice place to pull over. When they parked, he leapt out of his side and around to hers and jerked her out of the car. As she giggled at him, he threw her over his shoulder and ran up the stairs to their room. He nearly snarled when he saw that his son and daughter were sleeping in their big bed.

"They missed us." He growled low, and she laughed. "Come on and help me put them to bed. They'll be more comfortable there anyway."

Khan knew he would be as well. His daughter had a habit of sleeping on his head for some reason, and he had to peel her off every time she ended up with them. Carrying their son to his room, he tucked him into the bed and kissed him, then did the same for his sister. She yawned and looked up at him.

"Daddy?" She was getting better at saying it all the time. "Lub yous." She rolled over and he froze into place. When Monica touched his arm, he looked at her.

"She said she loves me." Monica smiled at him. "Please don't tell me that's not what she said. She said it."

"Well, I should hope so; I've been teaching it to them for weeks. Khanny can say it as well, but she never would. I think she gets her stubbornness from you."

He took her hand as she led them from the nursery. His daughter loved him. He smiled when he thought of all the time he'd been spending trying to get Khanny to say that he loved his mom, and realized that together he and Monica were trying to make them talk. He took her to their bedroom and pulled her into his arms.

"I love you very much, my wife."

She snuggled against him. "And I love you very much, my husband. Now get your ass naked and spread out on that bed. I'm going to show you just how much I do love you." His cock nearly hurt him when she ordered him like that. And who was he to argue?

Chapter 11

Wanera noticed the changes immediately. There were more beings saying hello to him than ever before. And they had taken to wearing name tags, names like "Tom," "James," and "Ken." He no longer called them beings unless he hadn't figured out their name yet.

He also noticed that he was sleeping better. He didn't want to say it was the new mattress, but he was sure that was part of it. He also had silk sheets, something he'd never had before, as well as a television. He smiled when he thought of the last two evenings with Bill. They had been together every night since they'd gone to get the computers together.

He went into the epicenter, which was what they called the room with the computer, and sat down on one of the many chairs to see what they had loaded this time for his amusement. He was beginning to enjoy the station called YouTube. He especially liked the shows that involved dogs and their tricks.

"My lord, the faerie has not been to the pizza place for many days. Do you think that she has been terminated?" It took him several seconds to realize that Bill had meant fired, not killed. "She is mostly in the computer place where we have been."

He nodded. "Perhaps she just took another job to be closer to her mate. I would if I were her. It's comforting to have someone you know close by."

Bill flushed when Wanera winked at him. He wasn't sure what possessed him to do something like that, but he enjoyed the man's company a great deal and was learning a great deal from him.

When the door slammed open behind them, Wanera stood and pushed Bill behind him.

"She comes, my lord. Mistress comes."

Wanera looked down the hall and could see his boss coming toward him. He looked at Bill.

"You have to hide. You know that she doesn't like you." Most of the beings disappeared just as his boss, Lady Darkness, came through the door.

"What the fuck is going on around here? I'm gone for a few decades and it looks like you've made changes to everything I liked. And what the hell is up with all these name tags? They mean nothing to me. Get rid of them." Five beings ran from the room and he watched them with his eyes, wishing he could go with them. "Aren't you going to offer me a seat, Wanera? And a drink?"

He pushed the computer chair he'd been sitting in moments before to her and then went to find someone to get him a bottle of something for her to drink. Bill usually took care of this and he'd sent him away. The moment he stepped through the doorway to see what he could find, he heard a whisper of his name. Bill was standing there with a large glass in his hand.

"Thank you." Bill nodded. "Find the others and tell them I'm sorry. Then all of you stay hidden. Hide in my room if you must." He turned back to the epicenter and handed her the glass, then sat in the other chair across from her as she sipped.

"You've been busy spending money, I see." He looked at the computer she was glaring at. "What on earth do you need something like this for? Does it kill things from here?"

"No, mistress, it does not." He nearly told her about the videos they'd been looking at when he realized she would find no humor in them. "I've been using it to find information on...on bad guys."

"And what have you found?" She leaned forward in her chair, and he was sickened by her odor. "There has to be something if you've spent all this money."

At random he clicked on one of the icons that he'd asked Bill about yesterday. He thought this one was the database to the police station. He was glad when he saw that when it opened, it was just that. He showed her how they were able to follow the most heinous crimes without leaving the room.

"Some humans have no regard for the law, and that's just...." He'd just caught himself from saying that was just horrible. He let her think whatever she wanted as he clicked on other parts of the page.

When had he changed? He knew that he had and wasn't unhappy with it. He wasn't lonely anymore, and he laughed. He tried to remember, before he'd gone to see the male faerie, when he'd slept so well and had been so...well, he was happy. He realized she was speaking to him and turned back to her.

"I asked you if you'd found a bride to breed with. Last time I was here you were saying that you were looking. Well?" Wanera decided at that very second that he didn't want a bride that he didn't know to come there. "Well, asshole, I'm speaking to you."

"No. I've been looking, but there doesn't seem to be many brides out there that would come to live in this realm with me." Sad but true. "I've decided that I might retire before my time is up."

She stood so quickly that the pain in his chest was secondary to the shock of her advancing on him. He lay there with his chest bleeding, wondering what had happened. She jerked him up by his throat, and he was glad for once that he didn't need to breath.

"You listen to me, you fucking poor excuse for a demon. You find you a bride and bring her here. I want you to bring several of them so that one of the fucking bitches will breed and live long enough to sire you a child. I will not be thwarted on this, do you understand me?" He tried to nod but couldn't, but she must have seen something. "You'll do this or so help me, I'll kill you myself by peeling every inch of skin off you an inch at a time."

He was thrown across the room and hit the crates that were being loaded with the older computer and things that they no longer had uses for. When she came toward him again, he curled into a ball, afraid that she was going to start now on killing him.

"If you do not have a bride here within a month, I'm coming back here and killing you. And when I do, I'm going to kill each and every one of your little beings until I get to that little cock sucker that I hate more than I do humans." She kicked him again. "Don't think that I don't know that you hid them away."

He didn't move but lay there as she kicked him half a dozen more times. By the time she left the room, he was hurting so badly that he almost wished for death. He looked up when Bill and a couple of others came into the room.

"Don't let her find you." Bill said she was gone. "I have only a month to find a bride or she's coming back to kill us all."

"We will find you one." Nodding, the men helped him to stand and then walk down the hallway to his room. Bill helped him try to get onto his bed, but Wanera hurt so badly that he ended up in a chair to rest.

"I can't do this," he told Bill after the others left. "I don't want to be here anymore. And I don't want a bride that I don't know. She'll hate it here. She'll die."

"What will you do, my lord? There is very little left that you can do but to do as she wishes." Wanera nodded. "If I can find you a suitable being, would that help?"

"No. I need a faerie. She would be the only being that could survive me. I need someone strong so that our coupling doesn't kill her." He closed his eyes, depressed. "I wish I could go and live with the humans. I know now that they aren't nearly as bad as we are taught they are."

Wanera sat there for several minutes before he heard Bill and some others return. They helped him get to his bed, saying he'd be more comfortable. Some of the others had his television from the sitting room with them. With him lying against the headboard of his bed, they turned it on and then settled around the room to watch it with him. Soon someone shouted "popcorn" and they began putting cupfuls of it in a bowl and heating it with their breath. There was enough popcorn in his carpet alone to feed a great army.

By the time they were all asleep, Wanera had made a decision. He was going to save as many of them as he could, starting with Bill. He closed his eyes again as the television went black, and tried to think how one got beings like his to a safe place.

~~~

The knock at the door startled Ama. Sebastian had left an hour ago and she was getting dressed to go and have a day with Monica and the other women of the household. When she bid the cook to come in, she was worried at once something had happened.

"Oh no, miss, I'm fine. Right as rain, but there's a...well, miss I'm not sure what he is. He said to tell you he comes in peace. I don't rightly know what he means by that, but he held up his four fingers in a sign that I don't understand."

After making sure the cook was all right, she went to the kitchen where...well, she wasn't sure what he was either.

"Hello." The little man jumped down off the chair and lay on the floor. She wasn't sure what to do, so she asked him to stand. He was making her nervous. She heard a car pull into the drive just as she got him to stand.

"I'm Bill." He grinned at her. "You're much prettier than a white blip on the computer. And a whole lot bigger, too."

"Thank you, I think. Why don't you have a seat and tell me what you need from me?" He nodded and climbed up onto the seat. She wanted to just pick him up and put him there like she'd seen Khan do with his children, but felt that it would more than likely hurt his feelings. She realized then that he was in a suit. A tiny little three-piece suit.

"My master is in grave trouble." She nodded and sat down. "I have come to ask you for your help in this matter before he's killed."

The door to the kitchen opened and Corrine and Monica walked in. They must have been forewarned about the little man, because neither of them seemed too surprised to see him. She introduced him to them.

"He was just telling me that his master needs my help. Do you mind?" Corrine started to say something, but she only closed her mouth and shook her head. Monica smiled and sat down across from her.

"The Lady Darkness has said that he needs a bride within the month, and if he does not have one, she will peel his skin from him an inch at a time. I do believe she will do this. She was most upset with him when she left." The little man looked around the room. "Would it be possible to have a cup of something hot? It is very chilly in here."

A shiver of something akin to fear rolled over her. "Chilly? I think it's about seventy in here. Just how hot do you like it?" He didn't answer but nodded when she asked him if he wanted hot tea.

"You're a demon servant, aren't you? A minion?" Ama nearly dropped the cup she'd just taken from the cabinet when Corrine asked him. "I've seen your kind in books. You serve a demon or a lesser demon."

"I do, mistress. I am servant to Lord Wanera." He took the tea bag from her as she stood with it, nearly to the table. "But I believe he is becoming my friend as well."

"Does he know that you're here?" Monica looked at her, then took the tea kettle away from her and sat in the chair. Ama was still trying to absorb the fact that the man who wanted to breed with her had sent one of his minions.

"No, he does not." The little man stared at her, then looked away. "He does not want you to come to the underworld, my lady. He has had a change of heart."

"Why?" He looked at her strangely. "What's changed his heart? A few days ago he came to my mate's place of business and offered to buy me from him. What would have made him not want me now?"

"The Lady Darkness. She came to visit him yesterday and beat him badly. And when she gave him that order to find a bride, he said that he would rather live with the humans than to subject one to live as he does. She has given him one month. If he has no one, she will kill him." He took the cup from Monica and smiled at her. "I have never had hot tea before. Is it good?"

"I suppose. I don't care for it myself. Why does he need a bride? I've heard that he needs a child so he can continue with his job. If he doesn't find one, then he's killed?"

Bill nodded and frowned. "Not entirely true. He will die, but it will be over the period of time he has reigned as lord. For my lord that would be about…seven thousand of your years. She will take that long to kill him. He heals, you see. Not quickly as you do, but he heals. She will wait until he is healed enough. Then she will begin again. I can only imagine what horrors she has in store for me. As I have said, she dislikes me a great deal."

"And now you come here hoping we'll help you?" Monica shook her head. "I don't know why you think we'd raise a hand to help a demon, but I have to give you credit for trying."

"You love him." Corrine startled them all by speaking. "You're in love with him and you're here to save him. That's right, isn't it? You're in love with your boss."

"I have been for many years. It has only been recently that he has come to be my friend. I do not wish to lose him so soon after he has made such changes in our lives." Bill took a sip of the tea and smiled. "This is very good. So sweet, too. May I have the recipe? I believe my lord will enjoy this as well."

Ama looked at Monica, who stood there with a glass of tea in her hand. She reached for it and drained the glass and asked for more. She and Sebastian had brewed three gallons of it last night, and she figured that it might be enough. By the time she was on her fourth glass, she felt she could talk to the little man. He grinned at her.

"You are a faerie and need the sweet tea to help you. You should also try standing with your feet in the dirt. It's very good for you as well. That is why you are named for the earth." He nodded and stood up. "I am sorry, my ladies, but I must go. My master is looking for me. I do wish you'd consider helping us."

"Helping you how? I'm not going to leave my mate, and I certainly am not going to have the demon's child. I like it here just fine."

He nodded at her and bowed. "My lady, all I ask for is a safe haven for him before the Lady Darkness returns to kill him." Then he was gone. She looked around the room and then stood up to pour herself another glass of tea.

"I forgot to give him the recipe for his tea." Monica sat down with the box of bags in her hand and started to laugh. "Christ, that was the strangest conversation I think I've ever had."

Ama had to agree. The man had actually asked for her to find a demon lord a place to hide. She looked at the chair he'd been sitting in and picked up the paper that lay there. It was a list of names and neat check marks by each name. She turned it over and read what it said.

"It's a list of names of beings. It says that the check marks indicate that they have been given a name tag. There are only two that have not. One called Benny and the other Jetts." She looked at the other two women. "They all have names of bands or cartoon characters from the television. Bill's full name is Bill the Cat. And here's one called Johnny Bravo."

Corrine started laughing. She was laughing pretty hard by the time Ama joined her. Then when Monica joined them as well, they were crying and laughing so hard they could hardly breathe. When they picked up the list again and began reading each name, they were nearly hurting from it. Then when the cook came into the kitchen and looked at them, shocked, the three of them started again. There didn't seem to be any name that was safe from the beings in the underworld.

Ama and the women went to the mall. They were just sitting down to lunch when Ama felt someone touch her mind. She frowned when she realized it was her father.

"I have been to your house to look for you." She wanted to tell him that she was a grown woman and didn't have to answer to him when he spoke again. *"There is the scent of demon all over your house. What the hell have you been up to?"*

She didn't want to answer him and decided that she wasn't going to. Looking over at Monica, she took out a pen and asked her to contact Sebastian for her and ask him to call on her cell phone. She took a deep breath before speaking to her father.

"I can do what I want, when I want. I haven't answered to you since birth, so I'm pretty sure your parenting privileges are revoked. And just what the hell were you doing in my house with neither Sebastian nor I there?"

She heard Monica speaking on her phone just as her father began to sputter and speak again. *"You'll not talk to me that way, young lady. I am still your father and you will respect me."*

"I most certainly will not, you pompous ass. If you can't speak to me any better than this, you can't contact me at all. If you do, then…then I simply won't answer you."

She wrote another note and asked if it was possible to block someone from contacting her. Monica nodded and told her to think of the person enclosed in a small room without any windows or doors and then walk away. Closing her eyes, she did that and felt the connection to him severed. Smiling, she took the phone from Monica when she handed it to her.

"My father is a shit and a pain in the ass. If he comes there, I hope you have him thrown out of your store and then have him arrested." Sebastian laughed. "I'm serious. If he comes there demanding to tell you how I mistreated him, you have to show him out."

"I will. Christ, I wish I could be there with you now. I bet your eyes are glowing as bright as an emerald." She looked down at her ring. "Want to play in the woods after I get home today? We could end up by the pond again."

She felt her body respond to the memory from last night. She looked at the other women at the table and flushed because she was pretty sure they could hear him. She told him that she had to go and closed the phone. She felt him touch her mind, and he told her he loved her.

"*I love you, too. I'm with your sisters and your mom. Can you behave?*" She looked at Jonny and Caitlynne as they joined the rest of them. "*Sebastian, I really love your family.*"

"*I'm glad, but they're your family, too. So don't try and pawn all of them off on me.*" He laughed. "*I'm sorry, babe, but my truck is here. If Daddy Dearest shows up or tries to contact me, I'll tell him to behave or I'll sic you on him.*"

She looked at Corrine. "You feel better now? Sometimes just talking to your mate can make a world of difference. I'm so happy he and you found each other."

"So am I. So am I."

Chapter 12

Wanera paced the tiny office again. Where had the faerie gone to? He wondered. It was a business day, wasn't it? And there were people within his walls that would purchase his things. He saw the woman come into the room again and sit down. He watched her closely this time. There was something decidedly evil about her.

When she took out a key and put it into a drawer, he walked behind her, glad that she couldn't see him. She took out a medium-sized box and set it on the desk. He was about to go back to his pacing when she suddenly stood up and went to the door and closed it. It wasn't that that had him waiting, but the fact that she locked the door and brought her purse to the desk with her. Yes, he knew then that she was up to no good.

The little key that she took off a chain around her neck fit into the box. When she opened it, he leaned over her shoulder and looked as well. Money, the human form of currency, lay in the box in neat piles. He was amazed at the amount in the box, and when she took it out and began putting it into more stacks, he sat down on the cabinet behind her.

She counted all the stacks, then took some of the larger denominations off the top of each stack and put them into another stack. When she had a considerable amount of money in the last one, she gathered up the money again and put it back in the box, locked it, then put it away. When she leaned over to lock the drawer again, he blew across the stack she'd left on the desk and counted the money there, also making note of the serial numbers on several of them. When she put the nearly five thousand dollars into her purse, he sat back and watched her put her purse away, then unlock the door and leave. He was still sitting there when the faerie came in ten minutes later.

Wanera wasn't thrilled about appearing before the man, but he needed his help. He knew as surely as he was sitting there that Lady Darkness wasn't going to wait the entire month. She was going to demand that he take a bride. He knew now why she was doing it. She would have to run the realm if he did not find someone to take over or have a child.

The large faerie looked at him. Wanera was sure he couldn't see him, but he didn't move all the same. When he sat down on the couch across from his desk after closing the door and locking it, Wanera thought the man was smarter than he had first thought.

"Bill came to see my mate yesterday." Wanera's whole body seemed to chill. "He asked her to help you. He told her that a woman by the name of Darkness was going to hurt you, and he wanted her to help you find a safe haven. He said…. Would it be possible to show yourself? This is a little weird."

Wanera materialized before him. He was still sitting on the file cabinet and liked the distance between them just fine. The faerie didn't move either.

"You're not going to attack me again?"

The faerie shook his head and said, "For now."

"I'm not here to take your bride. I've decided that I don't want her."

That hadn't come out right, and the man seemed to know it. He laughed a little and stood up. Wanera tensed but didn't move. When he went to the small white box in the corner and opened it, Wanera's curiosity got the better of him and he went to see what it was.

"It's cold." He stepped back from it, afraid of the thing. "Why would you have such a thing in here? You don't think to put me in that, do you?"

"No. I keep drinks in it. I like my drinks cold. I understand from Bill that you like things hot. I can give you a coffee if you'd like. It's all I have here." Wanera looked where the man pointed. "If you've never had it before, it could be a little much. Bill liked the tea that my mate served him. She'd meant to give him some to take back."

"Tea. Yes, he mentioned tea, but he never said where he'd gotten it." Now that he thought about it, he never said where he'd gone when he asked him either. "He visited your bride yesterday?"

The man nodded and sat back down. "He was there to ask for our help in keeping you and the others safe. That's why I've not tried to hurt you as yet. Monica and my mother said they believed him, as did Ama."

He'd given their names to him. He wondered briefly if he'd done that on accident and decided that he hadn't. The man was sharp. He bowed slightly before him.

"I'm Wanera, lord of the Ninth Realm of the Pits, master to thirty beings that serve me and counter of the dead." The man stood up and put out his hand. "You are offering me your hand?"

"It's a form of acquaintances. You shake my hand as I do yours. It's the beginning of a friendship." Finally, the man reached over and put his hand into his and showed him how it was done. "See, no harm done. And my name is Sebastian Jay Bowen, Panther and King of the Faeries."

Wanera staggered back. He was king? That wasn't possible, that wasn't...then his mate was the queen. He moved back further and stared at him. It wasn't until Sebastian shoved him into a chair and pressed his head between his knees that he felt that he might not pass out. He spoke to him as he was being held down.

"I didn't know. I had no idea that she was...none. I swear it, I never knew." Sebastian told him to shut up. "You have to believe me."

"I do now. Shut up and take deep breaths." He told him he didn't breathe. "Yes, you do. You wouldn't have nearly fainted if you didn't. Now do it."

He realized he was breathing and wondered about that. Maybe it was because he was in the human realm. He didn't know, but he sort of liked it. As he was feeling better, Sebastian let him up. He watched as the man paced.

"That strange human that works for you? She stole money from you today. I would think she's done it a great deal, because she seemed to have it down to a science. She took five thousand of your human money from you." Sebastian looked as if he didn't believe him. "First, you must know that no one can lie to you. Secondly, I have serial numbers of some of the currency. You should know that she cannot lie to you either."

He pulled out a ring of keys and put one in the drawer, as the woman had, and then took out the box. He counted the money much faster than she had, then looked at him. Wanera was afraid he was going to blame him for it.

"There was nearly twenty thousand dollars in here last week. Now there is less than five thousand. I'd say you were right." He put the money back. "Where did she put it, do you know?"

"Her purse. She stuffed it in the front pocket. She's taken a great deal from you then?" Sebastian nodded and Wanera put a sheet of paper in front of him with the numbers on it. "I am sorry. If I had known earlier, I would have told you."

"I have to call someone. And now before she leaves, but I want to finish talking to you. I've talked to my mate and she said she wants to help you. She said that you need help and we have to help you. Besides, she liked Bill." Wanera nodded and stood when Sebastian picked up the phone. "Wait. Please just give me one moment."

Wanera paced the room as he spoke to someone named Caitlynne. Whoever this person was, they were coming down now. Sebastian told her to hurry. Wanera turned back to him when he said his name.

"I need a way to contact you. How do I do that?" Wanera had thought this might happen, that the man would want to see him again if he didn't kill him. He took a deep breath and marveled at how good it felt.

"I can give you something that I've never shared with anyone before, except my beings…my friends. It will give you access to my realm that no one else has ever had before. What I do for you will get me killed. You must know that." Sebastian nodded. "The last time I was here you drew my blood. Do you have a mark on your hand, the one that held me up?"

Both he and Sebastian looked at his hands very closely and there was no mark. Wanera took Sebastian's hand and held it in his own, both palms up. He looked at him once more, hoping that he wasn't making a mistake.

"You can trust me. I swear to you that you can trust me."

Wanera nodded and pulled a blade from the air. "I give you my mark, not as ownership, but as friendship. You will share this with the one true love of your life and no other." The blade cut deeply into his palm and blood oozed from it. "Take it freely."

"I take it freely." Wanera didn't know why he wasn't surprised by the fact that Sebastian knew the right words and when to say them. He poured his blood into Sebastian's palm and watched as it absorbed into his hand. The mark it left there was small in comparison to the amount of blood. And when he closed his hand, Wanera looked up at him.

"If I am killed, the blood will pour from your hand as if you're wounded and the mark will disappear. All you need to do is think of me when you look at it. It is a way for you to summon me. My death will be the only thing that will keep me from answering." Wanera took a step back and was startled when Sebastian grabbed him and hugged him. He tightened his arms around him and hugged back. It was the first time he'd ever been hugged in his entire life. Then before he could say anything more, he willed himself back to his own realm.

~~~

Sebastian watched as Debby squirmed in the chair. He liked watching Caitlynne work. It was fun to see her in action. Debby kept looking at him as if she expected him to help her. Well, kiddo, he wanted to tell her, you're on your own.

"Did you take the money?" Debby shook her head at Caitlynne again. "Then what if I told you that we have you on camera that you did? And a list of the serial numbers on file? Would your answer be different if I asked you that again?"

"You don't have those things. I work here, remember?" Caitlynne nodded at him, and he handed her the sheet of paper. "What's that? If you think to use a blank sheet of paper to scare me into saying something that will make me look guilty, you're as stupid as he is."

Sebastian's burst of laughter made them both turn toward him. Caitlynne had warned him to keep quiet, and he put his hand over his mouth. He might have been stupid, but he wasn't any longer. Both he and Caitlynne knew that Debby couldn't lie to him, but they were saving that for when the other cops showed up. And a few seconds later, three of them, including a female officer, showed up.

"This woman has a purse in her possession. I would like it searched for possible theft." Debby stood up and held her purse to her like a shield. She looked ready to bolt, but one of the officers stood in front of the door.

"You can't look in my stuff. I know that law. You need a warrant or something. And I know you don't have one or you would have showed it to me already. You don't have anything on me." She sat down and sneered at him. "You're going to regret this. I'm going to sue you for everything you have."

"I don't need a warrant to search your purse, Debby. When you signed on here, you signed an agreement that there may be bag searches if necessary. You agreed to them by signing your name." She was shown the paper. Then Caitlynne handed it to the senior officer. "So we're going to do a bag search right now. Hand the nice police officer your purse or we'll take it from you."

"You can't do this." Debby looked at him. "Please don't let her do this. I haven't done anything wrong. Nothing." She struggled with the cop taking the purse. "I'm your assistant. You couldn't run this place without me. I'm here more than you are."

Sebastian looked at Caitlynne, who nodded. "You might have been my assistant, but that gave you no right to steal from me. And you did, didn't you?" Debby backed up a step, fighting him. "You stole from me. You took out my cash box and took money, didn't you? How much did you take? How long have you been stealing from me?"

"I took...please don't, Sebastian." He asked her again. "I took nearly fifty grand over the past six months. I was going to pay it back, but you never seemed to notice so I took more and more. I was trying to stop it, but I knew that if I could win just one ticket, one big payoff, then I could pay it all back. But the stupid tickets never seemed to be in the right order. I never got a break."

"Lottery tickets?" She nodded at him. "You stole fifty grand to buy lottery tickets? Christ, if you had asked, I would have gotten you help."

"I don't need help," Debby snarled at him. "I have this under control. I can quit whenever I want. I just needed to pay you back, and then I would have had to make enough to live on for the rest of my life. And it would have paid off, too, if you wouldn't have caught me."

"It's here, sir. All the money you said was missing. There is also a list of what appear to be credit card numbers and expiration dates." The officer showed it to her boss, then Caitlynne. "I believe there is money here that might have come from today's sales as well. There are three one hundred-dollar bills. Should you count your drawer out?"

His money was taken into evidence, and Debby was taken away, still screaming that it was his fault she was caught. He wondered if she would ever own up to the fact that she needed help. Caitlynne sat down opposite him and sighed.

"That was fun." He chuckled at her. "You know that in the past few days, I've arrested a doctor and a clerk, and I don't even work for this town yet?"

"Yet?" She nodded. "You took the job? That's fucking awesome. The best news I've had all day. Congratulations. Is Walker happy?"

They were moving back within the next month. They had decided to keep the house in DC for other things, but to move back here for good. He was excited. She'd been offered the chief of police job last week. The man who did it now was retiring soon. Of course, she'd have to run for it if she wanted it next term, but she would be a shoo-in. The life as a CIA director was too boring for her, she said.

"He's thrilled. Khan and he have been working on the clinic set up as well. They are spending a great deal of time together. It leaves me enough time that I can get to know my newest sisters-in-law. I like Ama."

"Me too." She laughed. "The doctor? Did that pan out like you'd thought it would? I know that Doris was a little afraid to help you."

"She did really well. When she realized that all the nurses in the room with her were agents, she relaxed a bit. It also helped her to know that the meds he was going to put into her had been approved by Walker. She was getting a good dose of vitamins, not the shit he'd been giving her."

Anderson had been feeding her aspirin. Heavy doses of it, too, nearly ten times what a normal dose would be. The babies were simply bleeding to death from it, and her body was reject them. Aspirin was pretty lethal to all paranormals anyway, and to unborn children, it was toxic.

"I read in the paper that several more women have come forward. That has to help in the case." She nodded again, and he thought she looked distracted. "What is it? Something wrong?"

"Why do you smell like you've burnt something?" She got up and leaned over him, careful not to touch him. "You do."

Sebastian leaned back in his chair. He had to tell her because he liked her and he needed to talk to someone. She looked at him with a raised brow, something he noticed that Walker did a lot, too.

"I've been talking to a demon." She sat back down in her chair and crossed her arms over her chest. "It's not what you think."

"Since you don't know what I'm thinking, why don't you enlighten me? And just so you know, I heard about the visit from Bill the Cat." They both started laughing. "Next time you see him, ask him where the names came from."

"I will." He told her the entire story with the exception of the blood. He was still trying to work that one out. He looked down at the small mark in the middle of his palm and tried not to think about what it resembled. He was sure it wasn't a pitchfork.

"So you don't know what help he needs?" He told her no. "Then he could want you to give him Ama long enough for her to have his kid."

"No, he said he didn't want her. I believed him. He seemed...I was going to say he seemed scared, but I think he really was. Especially after he found out about the king and queen stuff." She nodded. "If you want to know the truth, it scares me, too."

"Me too. I mean, I love you both to death, but I have all sorts of problems with thinking you guys are going to be required to leave us as soon as this thing with Wanera is over." He and Ama had thought of that, too. "When is the ball thing?"

"Next week." He smiled. "We've been practicing with our wings. They're pretty neat. Not terribly useful, but neat. I think little George got the biggest kick out of it. And I swear to you we didn't take him off the ground."

They had been playing with him in the yard and Ama had taken off while he held little George. He'd laughed so hard he'd nearly made himself sick. When they took him home, he'd jabbered to his parents that he had "flyed." It took them twenty minutes to assure Walker and Caitlynne that they hadn't "flyed" with him anywhere.

After he'd agreed to give her a statement in the morning, she went home and he walked around the store. Trevor watched him closely but never said anything, and he wondered if Trevor thought he was next, or that Sebastian might think he had helped Debby steal from him. It was nearly closing time when Trevor finally approached him.

"Is she coming back?" Sebastian shook his head. "Good. Sorry, boss, but she was a bitch. I've never worked with a more controlling, lazier person in my life."

"She was all that. I had actually been thinking I needed a change of management anyway. You wouldn't know who'd want the job, would you?" He hoped that Trevor wanted it but didn't have a clue. "The pay sucks and the hours are long. But there is one perk."

"Oh yeah, what's that?" Trevor smiled. "Is it that whoever takes it gets to be your number-one guy? Or is it something like we get to be best buds and I get to be invited to that nice house you have?"

"All the above." They both laughed and Sebastian smiled again. "Nah, the perks are that this person would get a bigger discount, and if he proved to me that he wouldn't sit behind the counter and order others around and would actually sell,

I'll give him a percentage of his sales. But that part would be a perk, not for everyone."

Trevor nodded. "And if I knew someone who wanted this job…when would he start? And how much more is the pay?"

Sebastian asked Trevor what he made now. He had accountants do the payroll stuff for him so he really had no clue. When he told him, he looked around the store.

"I'll expect him to work as hard as he does now and he'll have to be trustworthy. Because as you can see from what happened today, I don't put up with thieves." Trevor nodded. "I could probably pay a good assistant manager…ten dollars more on the hour. But I want to make him understand he has to be worth it." He thought about how many more hours he was going to have to put in because he was short one person. "And as soon as possible to start."

"Good. I'd hoped you say that. And I can start tonight. If you want me." Sebastian smiled. "You do, I take it."

"Oh yeah. And so you know, I would have gone twelve more bucks an hour." Trevor smiled.

"So you know, I'm going to make more than that in sales for you. So stick that in your hat." After agreeing to some smaller terms, Sebastian had an assistant that he liked and one he was sure was going to double his sales in a matter of days. He went home after they closed together, already making plans to start interviews in the morning. Life was good all of the sudden.

Chapter 13

Wanera was still sitting at his desk over an hour after he'd told everyone he was headed to bed. He couldn't believe that he'd nearly gone to the human world and taken the queen of faeries for his bride. What an idiot.

The knock at the door had him picking up his pen so he could at least pretend he'd been working. When Bill walked in, he put it down on the desk and smiled at him. Bill sat in the chair across from him and smiled.

"You know." Wanera nodded. "You are not mad that I went to talk to the lady faerie? She was most pleasant to me, and she is the one who gave me the tea. I so wish I had gotten the recipe. You would have enjoyed it."

Wanera had had Sebastian write down what he had needed to get, and the man had given him the tea bags. He had even told him how to mix it up. Apparently there was a steeping issue that some people didn't get.

Wanera handed his friend the little box of assorted flavors and the container of sugar. He'd even been gifted two mugs with the name "Bowen Computers" with a little computer on the side.

Bill was so happy that he told him they would have to try to make it. Wanera pulled the little notepad out and told him how to go about it. Sebastian had been surprised that he'd written it down, but he had wanted it to be right. Wanera hadn't said anything but he had a feeling that soon he'd have to either sell his little friend or hide him in the human world. He had a feeling he, himself, would be dead within the month.

The first cup of tea hadn't turned out so well. The water had been hot, but they had poured it over the tea bag a little too close to the fire, and the little handle thing that hung outside the cup had caught fire and nearly singed both their brows off before they got it out. With the second cup, they'd been a great deal more careful.

They each had three cups. It had taken them to the third cup to figure out the sugar. The first cup after the fire they'd put in five tablespoons, and nearly had their bodies go into sugar fits. The second they'd only put just enough to fit between their thumb and finger, and had added little pinches until they liked it. The third cup they had put in one tablespoon and had loved it. They made a list for the next time one of them was in the human world.

"I like the chamomile. But I don't care for the orange tangy. It's much too...I'm not sure. But I like the Earl Gray, too." Bill nodded as he wrote it down. "Oh, and I don't know about you, but the raspberry smells really good. Let's try that the next time."

"Do you think there are more flavors? I bet we could look it up." They ended up in the epicenter and were laughing at some of the blends that people came up with. They both decided that they wouldn't care for milk in their tea, and maybe they would try a lemon slice. After debating about it for several hours, they ended up ordering several boxes of tea from a website, as well as several mugs that they both liked. And, of course, they had to get mugs for all the others, too.

He was headed back to his room when he turned to Bill. "Thank you for this. I didn't realize that I needed a friend so badly until you walked in the door."

"You are very welcome, my lord. It was most enjoyable for me as well." He stood there for a minute. "Sire, do you think she will wait the entire month that she gave you?"

"No. I think she'll be back here in the next couple of weeks. And in the morning, I'm going to make plans for all of you to go to the human world. Especially you. I don't want her hurting you, and we both know that she will." Bill nodded. "The man from today that I visited and the woman who gave you tea? They are the king and queen of faeries. I know that they will keep you safe. I know it. He gave me his name, and I gave him my blood."

"You did?" Wanera nodded. "That means he can come and go…you think he will harm us, my lord? Do you think he might be like Lady Darkness?"

"No. No, I don't. I think he is so far different from her that they would be mortal enemies if they were to go to battle. And I would bet that the king would win. He would have goodness on his side, something we don't see a great deal of down here."

"From you we do." That humbled Wanera. "You are a good man in a bad place. If you asked the Mistress of Darkness, do you believe that she would let you go?"

"No. Do you?" Bill shook his head. "She'll kill me. She doesn't want to come here and run this place, and if she has to, she'll kill me as payback. I really hate my life."

"Not your life, my lord. Never that. You simply hate where you are in it. But things will change. You'll see. Things have a way of working around to themselves." Bill nodded and walked away.

Wanera went into his room and thought that it might work around, but he doubted it would work in his favor. Rarely did things work that way. He went into his bedroom and looked around. There were things there that he'd been given over the decades. Things from his...what he now considered his friends, like posters they'd ordered, movies he'd never watched, as well as books. He had hundreds of books. He pulled one down now and decided to reread it just for the fun of it.

As he was settling down in his bed, he thought about what Bill had said. And he was right. He did hate where his life was right now, but wasn't really sure what, if anything, he could do to change it. Life wasn't about choices when you were a demon lord.

~~~

"Has he taken a bride yet? Or even tried to find him one?" Darkness paced along the floor and turned when the thing on the floor said something. "Sit up and speak so I can hear you. I swear to shit, you things are as useless to me as Wanera is right now."

"No, my lady, he has not. Neither found a bride or looked for one. There doesn't seem to be any activity of him going or coming from the human world at all." The thing dropped back down to the floor.

She couldn't understand what the fuck Wanera was doing giving his things names. It was the stupidest thing she'd ever heard of. Not to mention they were too stupid to remember them anyway. That's probably why they had on those ridiculous name tags, so that they'd remember who they were when he called them. Still, why call any of them to you when you could have one or two of them follow you around all the time?

She felt the air stir and had just enough time to back away when her boss stepped into the room. The thing she'd had in the room with her disappeared. She thought that he'd kill them, but the small scream still made her wince. She'd have to go and create more of them now. Always a time-consuming job. She bowed before him.

"My lord." She waited for him to give her leave to lift her head, but he only stood in front of her. After several minutes she began to think he was testing her, and stood as still as she could. Winning tiny battles with him was always a huge victory for her.

"You've been lazy." Her head shot up, then back down. "What have you done about the counts I told you I wanted doubled by the end of the period? I can tell you, nothing. There has even been a small decrease in counts."

Her mind scrambled and she could come up with nothing. She tried to think who was slacking, and no one was. All her subjects' numbers were up over last quarter by three percent. She was trying to think of a way to tell him this when he started to speak again.

"Wanera's numbers are the best so far. He had an overall increase by nearly ten percent. While your numbers have dropped almost double that over the past two quarters alone." She felt her hatred of Wanera boil over. "Maybe I should put him in charge and give you his realm. I know that you'd hate it as much as he does."

"He does, too. And he's named his things. I was there a few days ago and he's put name tags on them as if they were real. And he's not found a bride. Nor has he tried to find himself a replacement for when I have to kill him."

Her heart began to pain deep inside of her chest and she put her hands over the area, only to wrap them around the unseen hand around her throat. Then she felt herself being lifted from the floor. She closed her eyes when her face was level with his, his eyes blazing red and hot. She whimpered when he shook her.

"Look at me," he commanded, and she opened her eyes. "You think you're in charge now? You think you decide when one of my subjects would die? What gives you the right, nay the power, to think that you of all people would have the say in anything?"

He tossed her away and then stomped to her. Darkness curled in the corner around the broken desk and paperwork. He lifted her this time with his hand, higher than before as he tightened the grip he had on her heart. He was going to kill her; now he was going to simply kill her.

This time when he tossed her across the room, she went through a wall and hit the fireplace beyond it. Her body was broken in so many places that she doubted she'd be able to crawl from him, much less walk. When this time he picked her up, he did so by her leg and threw her harder against the stone of the fireplace. She lay there bleeding.

His finger came out and ran along her face. The searing pain ripped through her, but she could only whimper again. He'd broken her jaw and she knew that speaking was going to be out of the question until she had time to heal herself. When he stared down at her, she knew that he'd marked her as one that could not be trusted. The long line of a scar would never heal over, and her face, her lovely face, would be ruined.

"When I say something to you, you'll do as I say, not as you want. Understand me?" She simply looked at him, unable to do more. "Starting tomorrow you'll be replaced. I'm sick of your ways. And if Wanera names his beings and gets the results that he has, then perhaps all my subjects will need to follow his example. He gets the things I asked of him; you, however, do not. You are lazy and of no more use to me."

He stood up. His arms spread out and his dark wings fluttered slightly. But it was enough. The room's contents were suddenly aflame and all her things, all her dresses and boots, her hats and bags, all the things that she'd loved, were burning brightly. She watched as her silk sheets melted off the fiery bedframe. The television burst and the contents spilled onto the charred carpet beneath it. She would bet that everything in the other rooms was getting the same treatment. When the fires began to die down, he knelt down to her again.

"One day; you have twenty-four hours to get out of my sight and to the lower pits to work the coals, or I will do to you what you've threatened Wanera with." He smiled at her. "I hope you don't make the time, Darkness. The thought of peeling your skin off you an inch at a time, hearing you scream, begging me to end you, makes me hard as stone."

When he stood this time, he disappeared as quickly as he'd come to her. She lay there waiting for her body to mend itself, for all her bones to come together after being shattered and crushed, for her bloodied body to become whole again, the ragged cuts and tears to become seamless. She touched the open wound on her face.

"This is his fault. Wanera went to him and told him what I'd done." She sat up, still sore but healing much quicker now that the major injuries were healing. "I will not be put to work like a common whore. I will not serve this way, even if I have to throw myself into one of the hottest pits to avoid it."

It took her two hours to heal to where she could walk, and another three before she felt she could take on Wanera. The entire time she planned and worked out how she was going to take him down, thought gleefully on how he was going to scream and beg her for mercy. Her lips curled into what she hoped was a terrifying smile, and she thought about what she was going to do to that thing. The one that had dared all those decades ago to not acknowledge her when she'd walked into a room. He was going to be her first victim. That thing was going to regret the day that he'd ever met her. Both him and his master.

But first things first. She had to find her things. They hadn't all been killed by the master, she was sure of it. One or two would have felt him coming and hidden. She found one, injured, but not badly enough he couldn't crawl away from her when she found him.

"Get up." He pointed to his left leg, where most of it had burned off. "If you can crawl away from me, you can do what I want. Find me that thing of Wanera's that he treasures. The simpleton thinks that giving them a name will help him somehow, but I'll show his fucking ass."

"My lady, I cannot go to the other realm hurt. They will kill me." She flashed her heat at him before she could think. Killing him had been a great pleasure until she realized that now she needed to find another one and hold onto her temper.

The next one she found died as she was telling him what she wanted. So did the next one. By the time she found two hidden away in the counting room, they were so terrified that they had wet themselves. Disgusting animals.

"Get to Wanera's realm and find the one he uses the most. I think he calls him...." She shivered when she thought of putting names to her things. "I think he's called Dog or some shit. Bring him to me now."

They both disappeared, and she wished she could see Wanera's face when her things showed up smelling like they'd spent the better part of the day in one of the dung pits.

She was headed back to her rooms, or what was left of them, when she detoured to her office.

Here the room hadn't been touched. She figured it had to do with the fact that whoever her replacement was going to be would need the things here. She began opening file cabinets, pulling things out, and tossing them to the floor. The file boxes on the shelves were dumped and kicked around to make the files within scatter around. She was dancing on the last of the boxes when she remembered the awards she'd been given so long ago and tore them from the walls as well. She started to burn them but thought that he'd know, that the master would know that she'd burned them and come back. She'd come back in here just before the end of her time and set it on fire then. Maybe she'd put that thing of Wanera's in the middle and use him as the starter.

The rest of the night she found more things that had survived the master's anger. She was putting the last of the things in the room when she realized she was exhausted. Healing herself and being up all night had left her feeling like she needed a short nap.

Lying down proved to be more difficult than she'd imagined it would be. There wasn't a bed, and she had nothing else to rest her head on. She was just going to go to another realm when she looked at her face in the reflection of a glass.

He'd ruined her. The line that ran down her face from her forehead to her chin was about an inch wide and still seeped an oozy-looking liquid that she was sure wasn't blood. Touching the small discharge, she looked at it on her fingers and saw that it was dark yellow, about the color of pus. She backed away from her reflection and turned. There too was her ruined image, pus seeping now from her eyes and ears. Every time she turned there was another face to see, another place she was leaking from. Even her body began to be misshapen and bloated. Her full breasts sagged and look like they were losing firmness. Her waist, something she was very proud of, was no longer tiny and well-toned, but huge and seemingly moving with every step she took. She was ugly.

She looked around for something to cover her face with, but all she found was blackened things she had no name for. There were things everywhere, and she knew they were mocking her, laughing at her, and she kicked out at their charred remains. When she was running down the hall to escape, not even sure where she was headed, she saw the two things she'd sent to find Wanera's creature. She looked at them as they cowered away from her.

"What is it? What did you find?" The bigger of the two of them shoved the littler one behind him. As if that would save it, she thought. "Tell me now or you'll join the others in death. I'm not in the mood to fuck with you right now."

"You did this, mistress?" He looked around at the devastation before looking back at her. "You killed off all of us?"

She raised her hand to kill it but remembered she might need him. She lowered her hand and realized for a second that it hadn't flinched. He'd looked at her as if he dared her to do it. She clenched her fists, wanting to prove to it that she could and would do this if it drove her to it.

"We found nothing." She glared at it as it spoke. "Nothing at all. We looked for the one called Dog and didn't find him anywhere within the compound. Everything there is as it should be."

She snarled at it and it still stood its ground. She knew it was lying to her but had no idea how to figure it out. When she'd created these things when she'd first been created, she had made sure that they couldn't ever lie to her. And now she was sure this one had done so.

"What about Wanera? Where is he?" It shrugged. "What does that mean? You either found him or you didn't. Why didn't you bring him to me?"

"You never said for us to. You said to bring you Dog and we—"

"Stop calling him that. He's a thing, something that works for us and nothing more than that. Useless objects whose only purpose is to serve me and to obey me. You have no names because I have said so."

"My name is Oscar, and this is Donald. All of us have names. We gave them to each other so we'd be like the ones you seek. Wanera, their master, had allowed them to have them, so we wanted them as well."

Her flame hit it but nothing happened. She tried again and again before she realized it was laughing at her. It dared to laugh at her? She moved forward to destroy it with her hands, and he punched his fist at her face, hitting the wound and making her fall away. She watched them disappear from the room even as she heard them laughing at her.

Darkness sat in the room curled into a ball and tried to think. She couldn't do this alone. She needed some help to go after Wanera and bring him to her so she could kill him. She'd thought about simply going to his realm and getting him and that shit-for-brains thing he had, but she was reasonably sure that her powers were being drained away. She looked at the mark in her hand, the one that she'd received when she'd gotten promoted to the position she'd had until earlier, and saw that it was gone.

Closing her eyes, she remembered the day the master had marked her. He'd poured his blood over her head and covered her in it. She licked it in from her lips, tasting the power in it, and felt it run along her veins. The power was short-lived because he never shared himself with others, not in his bed like she wanted to be, unless they were very special. And he'd told her she wasn't, not by a long shot. Even she had never given her blood to anyone ever, not trusting that they'd not come to her lair and kill her for her riches. And she was rich. Human money as well as demon cash were hers for the taking once she'd been put into the position as overlord. And now it was all gone, burned to a crisp with all her other things. She wondered now why she'd never done what the other overlords had done and put it in the human world to use to escape to someday if need be. It was the one and only place that the master would not chase them to. He felt that to live among the humans for any amount of time would be punishment enough.

Darkness felt her body begin to relax and exhaustion take her. Soon, she knew she'd have to find Wanera and kill him, but she needed a nap more. Drifting away, she thought about killing the man. She was going to enjoy every second of it.

Chapter 14

Sebastian reached for Ama and pulled her body to his. She was warm and soft in all the right places and seemed to snuggle closer to him with each breath she took. He nipped at her bare shoulder and felt her shiver beside him. Biting her a little harder, he rocked into her ass.

"Sebastian, you're as hard as stone." She moved back against him. "Would you like me to help you with that?"

He moaned and rolled her to her belly with him over her. She was wearing one of his shirts again, which he found that he loved. Moving it up her body, he adjusted himself until he was able to bare her whole back, and then ran his hand up her skin.

"You feel like silk to me." She arched her back up like a cat, and he heard her purr. "Ama, purr for me again. I want to feel it this time."

Her body vibrated under his hand, and he leaned down and kissed her spine. She was moving under him in such a way that he knew she was close to coming. He nipped at her shoulder as he slid his hand around under her and into her pussy.

"So wet and hot." She moaned again and rode his fingers. "I want to feel you come this way, while I ride this pretty ass. Come for me, baby, and I'll make love to you slow and easy."

Her release rolled from her. It was a soft feeling compared to the other releases she'd had. This one was a long continuous moan that took his breath away and made him want more. As she shuddered under him, he continued to play with her, in and out of her with each downward stroke of her body. When she turned to look at him, he could see her love for him in her dazed eyes.

"I want you. I want to ride you." He nodded, unable to move from the need in her voice. "Let me, Sebastian. Let me sit on your hard cock and have my way with you."

He rolled to his back and watched her move. When she stood up at the side of the bed, he watched her strip out of his shirt and then slip her panties off. She touched her body and moaned, lifting her breast up and tugging at her nipple. He growled at her, his cock standing thick and ready for her. When she crawled over him, her breast just a breath from his mouth, he pulled her down so that he could sample her. She wrapped her hand around his cock and guided it to her wet heat.

He let her go and helped her slide over him and down to his balls. Neither of them moved for several seconds. He held her hips tightly over him while she cupped her breasts. When she rolled forward, he closed his eyes. Before long, it was too much, but he needed to see her enjoyment, so he opened his eyes to watch her.

She rocked back and forth without any rhythm. He wanted to help her, but his own enjoyment of her had him letting her find her own way. Soon, she was smoothing out, taking pleasure for herself. He knew that when she came this way, she was going to come hard and he wanted to watch her fall. The faster she moved, the harder he held onto her. Her hands suddenly spread on his chest and he felt claws bite into his skin as her cat roared to the surface.

Sebastian watched her fur race along her skin, while black, almost blue fur fought for control as her human side appeared as well. He moaned when the claws bit deeper and his cat snarled at him for release. He knew that if they were outside, he'd let him go enough to take her, but he couldn't in here.

Her movements became quicker, jerky almost, as she hit her sweet spot. Her breath caught and held, and he knew that this moment would be his forever. She arched her back nearly to his knees as she screamed. Holding her tightly, he leaned up and held her as she screamed again. Sebastian reached down and pressed his thumb hard against her exposed clit and watched her fall apart again.

He rolled her to her back and felt her legs wrap around him, and then took her hard and fast, thrusting his cock deep inside of her. He felt like he was home. Watching her face while she came again, he threw back his head and pounded in her as he came with her. His entire body seemed to need to race to the finish line first, and he dropped down and tore into her shoulder, a bite that had his mouth fill with her hot blood and give him a second, then a third climax that made his vision blur and his body quake.

Dropping on her, he lay there, unable to move for fear of shattering again. He knew that he was heavy but really didn't care at that moment. When he felt her giggle a short burst of sound, he shifted his head so that he could look at her.

"I'm nearly dead here and you're laughing. Would you mind telling me what you find so funny after the most extraordinary sex I've ever had in my life?" She giggled again, and he smiled at her. "You're so beautiful when you do that."

"You're an amazing lover. I wonder if I will ever be able to find—" He moved off her and pulled her over him and slapped her ass. "I was kidding, you giant baby."

They lay there for several more minutes, him just touching her wherever he could reach, and her letting him. When she lifted her head and rested it on her fist, he looked at her.

"I'm ready for you to share what Wanera gave you." He watched her carefully. Last night when he'd told her about it, she'd been upset with him, but when he'd pointed out that she had visited the little man and had waited to tell him, she told him he was right. Then he told her what the man had said and what he wanted them to do.

"Are you sure? I'm pretty sure that I can't take it back any more than he can." She nodded. "Okay. We'll do it."

The small knife that was lying on the bedside table had been there for a couple of days. They'd had cheese and crackers as well as some fruit that night, and had dropped the knife and hadn't been able to find it. It had fallen behind the dresser and wedged into the carpet. He pulled it to him now.

"What now?" He shrugged. "I guess he had a reason for giving this to you, right? I mean, who else do we know that can go between the realms without any problems? And if we can go there, it must not be as bad there as we've heard from my father."

The man had been to his store nearly every day since he'd been brought to their house. He'd smelled the demon on him and had told him he was making the biggest mistake he'd ever made in his life, and that he wasn't going to let his daughter be around such a man as him. Sebastian had thrown him from the store and into the street, telling him to stay the fuck away if he couldn't be helpful. He'd called his phone nearly hourly since and had even gone to see his parents. His dad had thrown him out as well.

"No one I—" Pain ripped through his head and he grabbed it. Then his ribs hurt like he was being kicked or beaten with a bat. His leg burned and he tried to rise up to put out what he was sure were flames that were taking over his body, but there was nothing. He heard screaming and realized that Ama was saying his name. He couldn't answer her as more pain, this in his head again, nearly made him black out.

His fingers began to bend at odd angles, and his arm suddenly snapped. He was sweating for the pain, and he was sure it was going to kill him. Over and over he heard a voice, a loud and angry female, and her manic laughter made his skin crawl. He saw Khan and his other brothers and thought they were holding him down. Screaming over and over, he tried to pull away from the pain, begged them to knock him out as his body began to break more, the pain overwhelming. Then he looked up and saw her.

A woman dressed all in black stood over him, a long nasty infected cut on her face. She kicked him again; his jaw broke under her boot. When she lifted her hand, he saw flames and knew that she would burn him. Flinching away, he saw a small man with fear in his eyes as he hid behind a piece of furniture.

Not his. It wasn't his house, wasn't his pain. When her hand lifted again, he knew what was happening. Wanera was being hurt, and burned. And the woman who did it was Darkness. She was killing him. Sebastian grabbed Ama as she held him and asked her if she took it freely. When she nodded, he ran his bloodied hand down her wrist to her palm and held it there. She answered him that she would take it.

"Find him. He's dying. Find him and bring him here." He fell back onto the bed and let the darkness, this one of his own making, take him. He knew that she'd help the man and no one would harm her.

~~~

Ama slipped off the bed once Walker said he was going to be fine. Fine? She wasn't sure how he could be, but they'd not seen him the way she had. The way his body seemed to bleed without anyone touching him, the way his hands and arms moved to odd angles that left him screaming in pain. She couldn't do anything but scream for his family to come to them. Come to her now and help him.

Khan had arrived first, his body sweaty and hot from his quick run there. He had pulled on a pair of boxers and nothing else, and he slammed into the room. Monica was only a few steps behind him. They had felt him, he said. When the first pain had torn through him, he and Monica had felt it and had come to him. They held him down, keeping him from flaying about and hurting himself more. When he grabbed her, Walker had just come into the room and threw himself over Sebastian as he screamed when his leg seemed to be burning off.

She nodded to them all as she looked at Sebastian. "I have to go to find Wanera. He asked me to and I'm going."

"No, you're not." Her father stood in the doorway. "If I have to hold you here in my arms, you are not going to go to that...lord, and touch him. Let him die. For what he's done, he deserves it."

Khan stepped up beside her, as did Reed and Marc. She felt the others, the other brothers, do the same. Her father took a step toward her, and Khan suddenly shifted and growled at him. Her father glared at him.

"You'll pay for this. See if you don't. Helping an underlord can only mean death for you, and I'm not going to be here when you return if you plan to go through with his insanity. Is that what you want? For your own father to leave you now that we're together?" Monica stood up and stepped in front of Ama. "You think you're protecting her? All you're doing is sending her to her death. Is that what you want?"

"Get out." She glanced at George as he and Corrine walked in the door. "Get off this property and never return. You're no longer welcome here. And if you come onto this land again, I will personally tear you apart and piss on you."

Her father took a step toward her, and a shift in the room was the only warning he got. George had shifted so quickly and smoothly that it had taken her breath away. Her father stopped moving. George looked like a frail man as a human, but as a panther, he looked like he could have had him for breakfast. Her father looked at her.

"You would choose them over me?" She nodded immediately. "Well, so be it. I hope that you can live with yourself after this. If you live at all."

When he left the room, she looked at the men and cats surrounding her. The women were standing near the bed, and she knew that if he had taken one step toward Sebastian, they would have killed him on their own.

"I have to go and get him. If for no other reason than to let him die here." Monica nodded and smiled. "Will you watch over him while I'm gone?"

"Yes. Khan and the others are going with you." Monica laughed a little. "I wouldn't try and keep them from going with you if I were you. I'm pretty sure that it might get you into deeper trouble than it's worth. And Khan wants to know if you could please pledge to him. He said he can help you more if you do."

She dropped to her knees and looked him in the eyes. "Your timing sucks, you know that, don't you? But if you can help me, I'm for it. I don't know the words because I can't think beyond the terror that I feel for that man on the bed, but if this won't work then we'll have to wait until I get back. I don't think Wanera has a great deal of time left."

He nodded at her, and she could see the man Khan in the eyes of the cat. "Khan Bowen, as my male and my brother-in-law, I pledge to you because I've never met a man more able to help when needed, more loving a man to his family, or a better friend to me. I give you my all."

He licked her throat, and she felt tears. Wrapping her arms around him, she held him to her as she cried. Monica came up behind her and put her hands on her shoulders. Ama pulled back.

"I'm sorry. I know I'm not supposed to touch him, but I needed...I'm sorry."

Monica patted her on the back, and she looked up at her. "That was the most beautiful pledge I've ever heard." She glanced at Jonny and Jack. "Those two made it sound like a threat, but he loved it. He wants you to look into his eyes to make the connection."

Ama looked at Khan again and felt it snap against her mind like he'd touched her. She smiled at him when he rubbed his massive head to hers. Standing, she looked around the room. This was it.

"Okay, you guys, we're off. Let's go and kick some ass and take some names." Reed shifted first, then Marc and Dylan. Dylan moved up beside her, and she touched his fur. As Walker shifted, she had a moment of panic that he was leaving Sebastian when he needed him, but Monica assured her he was just sleeping.

"We'll keep him safe. Won't we, Corrine?" Her mother-in-law nodded, and Ama realized that George was going with her. Before she could say she thought he should stay there, Khan touched her mind.

"He needs this." She nodded, and they all stood in a circle as she tried to think how to get them to Wanera. A swell of heat and a great movement—she opened her eyes and looked at the destruction.

The cats stood surrounding her. She knew that Khan was right in front of her, but wasn't really sure until one of them brushed by her that she knew who each of them were. She nodded toward a room that seemed to be the only one that had power.

She stepped over little men with tags on, some of them dressed in child-sized jeans and shirts, while others were only in shorts, all of them dead or near death. When she leaned down to one that wasn't hurt as badly, he shook his head.

"You must find the master. He will need to know what has happened." He laid back his head and smiled. "I have called to him for you."

She wondered who he meant and figured that he had meant Wanera. The poor man was hurting so badly that he seemed to be out of his mind with the pain. She moved closer to the light and was stopped by a half dozen or so men standing there with bats and large pieces of wood.

"I've come to see to Wanera. He and my mate are friends. He said...Sebastian said he was hurt. I want to see if I can help him." The men didn't move until she heard a voice deeper inside the room.

"Let her pass. She is the queen I was telling you about." She moved toward who she thought was Bill and found him holding something in his arms. "He protected me. And the others. He never told Darkness where we were, but we came out too soon, and she...she is an evil being."

Ama heard the cats snarl and turned to see the men trying to keep them from her. She looked at Bill. "They'll hurt them if they can't see me. Could you ask them to let them pass? They won't hurt them, I swear it."

Bill nodded and told them to let the panthers in. "He is hurt very badly, my lady. I do not believe that he will live. He protected us with his life, and now he will die because of it."

She nodded and looked down at the man. She knew what his injuries would be because of the ones that Sebastian had received from him, but her mate hadn't received everything. Wanera had been hurt probably ten times more than her Sebastian had been.

His body was burned all over, his hair was gone, and his face was ravaged with it. She wanted to touch him but wasn't sure where to touch him that wouldn't cause him more pain. She finally put her hand over his throat, the only part of him that seemed to be unharmed. Magic hummed along her skin, and she had a moment to wonder what he was doing when the cats roared. Several of the little men came running toward them and hid in a large hole in the wall.

The being that appeared with her had her cats snarling and growling. When it looked as if one of them was going to leap at the large creature, she stood and told him to stop. Reed turned to look at her. The others, their hair high on their backs, never moved. Reed came to stand in front of her as the being spoke.

"You run with a beautiful bunch, male. Where did you find such a prize?" The being looked at Khan. "You understand me and I will you. Speak and tell me why you come to my world unwelcomed."

Ama stepped in front of Bill and Wanera to shield them if necessary. No one was going to hurt either of them again. She raised her chin when he looked at her.

"The faerie queen, are you not?" She nodded once at him. "And what have you behind you that you would die for? Another cat? Someone who will pay for what has happened here today?"

"You'll not harm him again or I'll kill you myself." He raised a brow at her but said nothing. "They've been hurt enough by that bitch, and I won't have you harming them as well. Let me take Wanera and Bill back with me to—"

"Wanera has been hurt?" He moved so quickly she couldn't stop him. When she turned, he was kneeling on the floor beside the fallen demon. He touched Wanera's hand softly and looked at Bill.

"Who did this? You know...I demand that you tell me." She stepped in front of Bill. "I'll not harm him. I know now that you and your cats didn't do this, but I demand to know who."

"Darkness." He looked up at her, then down at Bill, who nodded. "She hurt my mate, too, when she hurt him. Her fucking ass is mine."

"He gave his blood to you." She nodded, even though he was no longer looking at her. "He is my creation. My first child, I guess you would call him. I had to...he couldn't be shown any favoritism from me, but he held his own."

"Well, of course he did. He's a good man, you moron." He looked up at her again and she flushed. "I'm sorry. My mouth gets ahead of my brain when I'm afraid and nervous. What I wouldn't give for a big glass of sweet iced tea right now."

It appeared in her hand and without thinking, she drank it down. When it refilled itself twice more, she nodded to the large man. He winked at her.

"I knew a faerie once long ago. He would suck the nectar out of flowers to get his sweetness. You should try standing in the earth. It will replenish you faster." She nodded and told him she'd heard that before. "Yet you've not done it. Why are women so stubborn?"

Before she could answer him with what she was sure would get her killed, he stood up. She looked at him and frowned. "You never gave me your name. I'm—"

"Do not, my lady. Giving a being like me your name is very dangerous. And I will keep mine to me as well. You may call me master if you wish." She looked at him and he laughed. "Okay, you may call me 'Sir.' I believe that is better for us both."

He looked down at Bill and Wanera. She knew now that he wouldn't harm either of them, and wondered what he'd do if she asked if she could take them back with her. She turned when the cats started snarling again, and a beautiful woman, probably another demon, snarled at them to shut up. She turned to Sir to see who it was when she realized he was gone.

"*Take them back with you to the human world. I will take care of the bitch for you.*" She nodded to Khan when he turned to her.

"*I'll take all of them then. Even the ones that are hurt please, to see if I can help them in memory of Wanera. He loved them very much.*" She felt his laughter and shivered from it. "*You'll let me?*"

"*Take them and all that belongs to Wanera. I will help you transport them with your cats.*" She started forward to gather Wanera in her arms when she felt Sir touch her mind again.

"You'll no longer be welcome here, my lady, but I may visit you to see to Bill and the others. Will that be acceptable?"

"Will you behave?" He laughed again and told her he would. "Then you are welcome in our home. Thank you for helping me. I'll make sure that Wanera is buried among friends."

He was laughing again as she felt the heat dissipate and light touch her skin. She opened her eyes to find herself in another bedroom in their home and several of the beings surrounding the bed. She left them to find out if Sebastian was okay. She knew that they would need their time to say goodbye.

Chapter 15

Darkness looked around for the cats. They had disappeared and she was somewhat disappointed she wasn't going to get to kill them as well. Taking a deep breath, she looked around at the destruction she'd caused in coming for Wanera. Smiling, she realized she could really get to like this kind of killing. Massive murder count and the feeling of being queen afterward. She went to the room she'd left Wanera in. Hopefully, he'd tell her where that fucking little prick of a thing was.

The large cat was sitting where she'd left Wanera. He looked vicious and ready to attack. She raised her hand, then lowered it again when she realized that she'd used up all she had, and now she was little more than a human. But he wouldn't know that.

"What the fuck did you do with Wanera? I want to see if the little shit is ready to talk." The cat snarled at her but didn't move. "You think you can take me on, big boy? Well, you just try it and I'll singe you so badly your own mother won't recognize you."

He growled but still hadn't moved. She moved more into the room but stopped when he stood. He was fucking huge, much bigger than she'd seen in a panther before. She took a step back and screamed when hot hands wrapped around her upper arms.

"Hello, Darkness." She closed her eyes at the voice behind her. She knew that voice as well as her own. Her master.

"Master." She nodded to the panther. "Is he one of yours? He'll be a lovely addition to your trophy room. I can't wait to—"

She snapped her mouth closed when the cat roared. His teeth were as long as her longest finger and as sharp as any blade she'd ever seen. She watched him as she walked toward her, but couldn't move because her master had yet to let her go.

The cat watched her with his dark eyes. There was no doubt that in her present condition he could rip her to pieces, but she stood still, barely blinking at him as he walked all the way around her. When he touched his nose to her hands, she whimpered.

"Do you know who this is? The cat, do you have any idea who he is?" She shook her head as he moved back and sat down not a foot from her. "He is the friend of Wanera, a trusted friend. They exchanged names and blood. How do you think it made him feel when you nearly killed his friend?"

The threat—because there was no doubt that's what it was—came from him as a whisper in her ear. She knew that the cat had heard him, too, because he snarled again and showed her all his teeth.

"I don't...I have no idea what you're—" Master shook her hard, and her teeth rattled in her mouth. She felt his hands burn into her flesh deeper, and she moaned from the pain.

"Lie to me again and this will go much worse than you can imagine." He shook her again, and then suddenly shoved her forward to the cat. "He is going to deal with you for his bit of flesh. Then I will take over. You'd better hope that he kills you, Darkness, because I most certainly will not."

Her body became chilled. He knew and not only did he know, but he was pissed about it. She turned to him to look him in the eye. Wanera couldn't mean that much to anyone.

"He was cheating. Did you know that? He had a computer set up to help with his counts, and he would be the first to get to them. I didn't have a computer, and I should have had it before him. Then I would have presented it to you as my idea. It should have been mine." She realized she was babbling when he raised his dark brow at her. "As his boss, I should have been the one to come up with the good ideas."

"You're very right about that. As a boss you should have, but you're too stupid and too vain to come up with anything." He leaned back against the wall. "I've talked to the others under you."

The hair on her arms stood up. She was afraid. If he talked to even one of them, she was as good as sentenced. She glanced back at the cat who watched her. Master's laugh made her turn back to him.

"He is thinking you might suffer more if I take you first." She looked back at the cat and decided he was her best bet if she wanted to come out of this situation dead. She looked back at the master.

"I served you well." He nodded. "And now you're going to give me to this cat to be killed, bloodied like I was nothing to you."

"You were nothing to me, Darkness. Ever. You were a poor manager, and worse yet, you never learned even after all the training I gave you. And according to some of the others beneath you, you're not even a good evil person." His body heated and started to shift before he seemingly got control. "But Wanera, for all the things you thought of as faults, had the loyalty of all the beings who worked for him, better numbers than anyone on your team, as well as their respect. He even, when needed, asked for help. Not from me, but from someone that could get him out of this place."

"What do you mean, out of this place?" She looked around and saw the cat down on his belly and his hair standing on end. "You can't mean that he's dead. He can't die. Not unless I say so."

"*You* say so? I hadn't realized that I'd given you that authority." He moved from the wall and walked toward the cat. "Not that it matters, but he's been given permission to leave here. It was the only way I could save my son."

Son? She stood there thinking about what that meant. If Wanera was his son, that meant she'd tried to kill…. "I had no idea. Master, you must forgive me in…"

"Take her." The cat lunged and she felt his claws rake across her face as soon as Master spoke. Even as her sight was blurred from her eye being torn from her, she could feel him tearing at her soft belly and her arms. Pain poured over her. She screamed over and over until she could no longer do so with the fangs tearing at her throat. Her body was torn up, shredded from claws and teeth, but still he attacked. When she heard the softly spoken, "Stop," she nearly wept, would have if she could have remembered how to do it from the pain pounding in her mind.

She must have blurred out, because as she opened her eye her name was being said. Master was standing over her, as was the panther. He was covered in her blood…it dripped from his mouth and fur. And when he snarled at her, she could see it on his teeth — they were stained with it.

"Darkness, look at me." She tried to turn to do as Master commanded, but she couldn't. "You should see what he's done. I do believe you've really made an enemy of him. Oh, and by the way, I lied to you. You understand that concept, don't you? It's where you don't tell the truth."

"Please," she begged him. She wanted it done, wanted this over with. Master shook his head at her and smiled. It didn't reach his eyes and she shivered, her body aching from the action.

"My new friend here is not the one you harmed, but his brother. He is here on behalf of Wanera and his family. Have you ever known a panther male with such control? I would have killed you outright, but he has decided to give that pleasure to me." He chuckled at her. "Not that I plan to kill you, but you'll understand shortly."

Power surged through her, and she could feel her body responding to it. The master was healing her, and she knew that while it would feel much better, she wasn't going to enjoy what came next. He handed her a mirror as he sat her up, and she held it before her face as he instructed her to.

"As you can see, I won't make you whole, but I will give you life." Her face was ravaged. Long streaks of scars, still wide open, marred her face worse than the one he'd given her. Her left eye was gone, and in its place an empty socket that seemed to be as dark as her name. Looking down at her throat, it was the same: long teeth marks now pink with healing, but no less ugly. The rest of her body was as bad. Her belly was scarred deeply. Long gaps of skin seemed to have healed over each other, and she had thick places that seemed like furrows in a garden. Her left leg had healed but at an odd angle, and she knew when she walked it would make her gait sloppy and give her the appearance of a drunkard swagger. She looked up at her master.

"I beg of you to kill me." He shook his head and stood up. "Please, I beg of you. I don't wish for others to see me this way."

"I'm sorry, did I give you the impression that I give a shit what you want? I do sincerely hope not." He lifted her up, and she staggered slightly. She thought that he'd help her, but he took a step back and glared at her. "You'll not touch me, you hideous creature."

She looked for the male cat, wondering if she attacked him again if he'd finish the job, but he was gone. Darkness looked at the Master as he moved to the wall again. She knew that this was where she'd find out her sentence.

"You'll spend all of eternity serving the men and women who work the pits. You'll give them new equipment when needed, and you'll be their entertainment as well as an example of what happens when I'm pissed off." She shook her head and started to beg, but realized that she could no longer speak. "The only words that will ever spill from your lips again will be 'yes, Master,' 'no Master,' and 'thank you, Master.' You'll never lie to anyone again. I give you leave to say one thing, the last thing you'll ever say."

She thought about what she'd done and what she now had to endure for more years, she had no doubt, than she'd been living. And she was nearing her third millennium. Darkness also knew that begging wouldn't help her. If anything it would piss him off more. She lowered her head and decided that begging might be her only recourse.

"Will I ever be able to redeem myself?" She felt the floor shift, and her body was suddenly thrown forward. Before she could catch herself, she was falling. When she landed, she knew where she was. She knew that she was never getting out of there, no matter how long she served him. The voice that thundered through her mind made her fall again, and she lay there for several minutes as the heat from the pits singed her skin.

He'd told her no. He'd said simply "*No*" as he'd thrown her away to the fiery pits that served him. Standing up, she noticed that her clothing had changed, too. She was no longer in the sexy little dress and heels she'd put on before leaving the underworld, but a shirt that was cropped at her waist to show her scars, shorts that showed her legs, and no shoes. Darkness turned to look at the fires before her and thought about throwing herself into them as so many had before.

"You do that and I will leave you there long enough to crisp your skin, and then pull you from the flames to fulfill your sentence anyway. Now get to work."

Picking up the first of many shovels and picks, she loaded them onto the cart. She was just starting to put the straps around her waist to drag the cart to the works when she felt a small stirring in her mind. She had a sudden thought that he was going to change his mind when an image of herself, beautiful and full of life, flashed before her eyes. As she stood perfectly still, more images filled her mind. She watched in horror as those were replaced with images of her now. This looped around several times before she realized that this was something else that she would have to endure. A slide show of her destruction.

Tears poured from her eye as she made her way to the first pit and handed the man standing there a shovel. He stared at her for so long that she wanted to slap him, but then he started laughing. As she moved on to the next pit, the same thing happened. They were all laughing at her and would, she was sure, for the rest of her days. Darkness was no more. In her place was this monster.

~~~

Khan watched his brother sleep. Sebastian was going to be fine, but he needed to rest. Everyone was making sure that he did. He looked up when Wanera and his friend, Bill, came in.

"Is he still sleeping?" Khan nodded. "I had hoped to speak to you and him together. May I please have a word with you then?"

"Yes." Khan didn't know how he felt about this man. He'd not been the true cause of what had happened, but Khan couldn't help but associate what he'd done, and what he'd do over again if need be, to Wanera and his group of men.

"I would ask that you help my friends while I go and try to speak to the master. I would like to be able to stay here and live among humans. I'm not...I don't believe I could go back and be the same as before. Especially with Darkness there as my boss."

Khan had told no one what he'd done. When he'd returned from the underworld, he'd told his mate that he'd had business to take care of. She had nodded, but he knew that she'd not believed him. He promised her that he needed to speak to Wanera and Sebastian first. She kissed him and told him to shower before he sat with anyone else, or they would know where he'd been.

"I don't think you'll have to worry about Darkness again." Wanera looked at him, and Khan shifted on his seat, reaching for the things on the floor before continuing. "I have something for you. I found it when I was returned here."

He handed him the large scroll and then the case that had been beside him when he'd ended up in Sebastian's yard. Wanera took them and handed the case to Bill. Neither of them spoke as Wanera broke the seal and looked at it. When he rolled it back up and handed it to Bill as well, he asked the man to give him a few moments.

"He has released me." Khan nodded, figuring that was what the larger man had done. "He said that I am to try and make my way in this world with the help of you. He said that I could learn a great deal from a man such as you."

"I don't know about that. I didn't do anything that any other man wouldn't have done when his family was hurt." Wanera nodded. "Did he tell you what happened?"

"He said that you avenged your family and me. He said that I am indebted to you, as is he." Wanera stood up and looked down at Sebastian. "He saved me through you. Had you not come—"

"You would have died." Wanera nodded, still looking at Sebastian. "What will you do? How will you live here?"

"I was given my money that I had in my lair. I also have a great deal here that Bill has stored for me. He has been doing it since I started working, and says that I have enough to be nasty if I want." He looked at Khan and smiled. "I'm not entirely sure what that means. Do you?"

"No. Sorry, I don't." Khan looked at his brother as he stirred on the bed and glanced at his watch. "His mate will be here soon to watch over him. Do you know how much longer he will sleep this off?"

"Soon." That was all he said as he moved toward the door, but stopped and turned back to him. "Master has told me that I owe him my life. I will repay him."

He was out the door before Khan could ask him how he was planning to do that. He looked at Sebastian when he said his name softly. Standing up, he moved to the side of the bed and smiled at him.

"It's about fucking time, you lazy bastard." Sebastian sat up but winced a little. Khan helped him until he was sitting and leaning back against the headboard. He asked him if he wanted him to get Ama.

"Not just yet. I have to tell you something. I've already explained things to Ama about what happened." Khan nodded. "It's about that man Wanera. He gave me his blood and I'm connected to him."

"We know." Khan laughed at Sebastian's look of surprise. "You've been asleep for nearly twenty-four hours, and in that time a great deal of shit has hit the fan. We've been to hell for you, buddy."

"Hell? I don't understand." He looked down at his hand, and Khan hid his own under his leg. "It's gone. The mark he gave me, the one that said…. Is he dead?"

"No. Not yet at any rate. But if he flushes the toilet again just to hear the sound and to watch the water, Mom might kill him for that. He's been resting, too, but he healed a little faster." Khan took a deep breath. "When you told Ama to go and save him, we went with her. There was no way I was going to let her go without some protection. It was a good thing, too. That bitch showed up. But so did someone called 'Master.' He told us to bring Wanera back with us."

Sebastian reached over and pulled his hand to him. Khan had noticed the mark when he'd returned to this world. Sebastian looked at the tiny little fork for several minutes before he spoke.

"It's not like mine was." Khan nodded. "It's redder and seems to be a little more detailed. Who gave this to you? The Master?"

"He never touched me that I can remember. But I'm pretty sure he did it for…." He looked away. "That woman, Darkness, she hurt you and the others simply by making Wanera hurt. She wasn't going to hurt my family without some sort of payback. But as much as I wanted to kill her for that, I couldn't."

"No, you wouldn't. You're a good man, Khan, and a better leader. But this mark...what does it mean? Do you know?" He shook his head. "Then we need to find someone who does know. Maybe we can ask Wanera."

Khan stood up. "I will, but for now I need to let Ama know you're awake, unless you've already told her." The door opened behind him, and he glanced at Ama. "I see that you have. I'm sure you two have plenty to talk about, and I have to go and tell the rest you're awake."

Khan left, knowing that neither of them heard a word he said. He was nearly down the stairs when he felt a small touch of someone and stilled. It wasn't his family, and it wasn't anyone he knew.

"*You've helped me with a problem that should never have been. I marked you so that others that saw you knew that you were protected by me.*" Khan leaned against the wall and tried to wrap his mind around the fact that he had been marked by this man.

"*I don't...I'm not really sure what you think I did for you, but there is no need for you to protect me. I was avenging my family, not helping you.*" He heard the laughter and shivered. It was not a happy sort of sound.

"*You are very strange, male, but I can respect your wishes. I have but a favor to ask of you. Neither a large one, nor does it involve anything more than you are willing to give me. I would like information on Wanera on occasion. Nothing much. Just to hear that he is...making it, I suppose.*" Khan smiled. "*You think my request funny?*"

"*No. I think it's a great request, but unnecessary. I think that Wanera will succeed no matter what he tries. He's a good man and a better being for what he's learned on his own. Having friends is one thing, but he never put his needs above his friends, even though I'm pretty sure he was supposed to."*

This time the man's laughter was just that, full of humor. Khan felt himself relax a bit. Maybe the man could see why he didn't need to be protected. But Khan had a feeling he was going to be stuck with the man.

"I will be very happy if he does do a grand job. As you have probably surmised, he is more than just an employee of mine; he is one of my creations. Darkness was as well, but she was...I was at a darker time in my life when I made her, so she didn't turn out as I had planned. But I can see your point. Wanera will be a success, and I will not mark you. You're a good man as well, male. One I am very happy to know. I will bother you no more."

Khan looked at his palm when the connection was closed. It began to fade almost immediately, and for that Khan let out a long, slow breath. He closed his hand over the now clear skin and moved to the kitchen to tell his family that Sebastian was going to be fine. He was also looking forward to going home with his mate and seeing his children. Also, he wanted to take his wife to bed. She was still in heat, and he wanted her fat with their child again very soon. Smiling, he entered the kitchen. Khan was a very happy man.

Chapter 16

"You're still dressed." Ama looked at him from the doorway and smiled. It was all Sebastian could do not to leap on her and take her right there. But while he was feeling better, he knew that he'd use all his energy if he did that, and wanted to expend what he had on making love to his mate.

"I am. What do you have on, Sebastian? It looks like you have more on than me." He sat up more and pulled his shirt over his head. "More. I want to see all of you."

"Come here and help me then." She moved away from the door and pulled off her own shirt and dropped it to the floor. "Ama, strip for me. Please? I want to see you naked and standing before me."

She stopped moving about halfway across the room and ran her hands up her sides to under her breasts, where she slipped her hands under her bra. He watched as her hands moved against the heavy flesh and felt his cock jerk to attention. She was going to kill him. When her bra slipped off her shoulders, he wanted to follow the tiny straps down to her elbows and then suckle at her skin as it was revealed. She held her hand over her nipples as she pulled her bra off and dropped it to the floor with her shirt.

"Don't tease me. Let me see them." She lowered her hands, and his breath caught. She was the most beautiful creature he'd ever seen. "I want to see all of you."

The pants were next, but she left her panties in place. He smiled. She was leaving them for him because he'd told her that he loved ripping them from her. When she stepped toward him, he moved his legs to the side of the bed and unbuttoned his pants. It was either that or his cock was going to strangle. When she was standing in front of him, he leaned in and kissed each of her hips.

"Do you have any idea what I want to do to you right now?" He kissed the area just below her navel, then swirled his tongue in the small indentation. "What I want to taste of you?"

"Yes. I want the same things. I want to feel your tongue inside of me. I want to feel your cock, too, as you fill me." She moaned when he turned her around and bit her ass. "Sebastian, I can almost come with you doing that."

He bit her again as he slid his hand to her front and into the small triangle of her panties. She was wet and hot, and when she opened her legs for him, he nearly sank his teeth into her deeply just to feel her come. He touched her hard clit, and she rocked into his hand. He turned her back around and buried his mouth over her.

"Sebastian." His name ended on a moan, and he curled his hands into her panties and jerked them off her and suckled her clit into his mouth at the same time. She came quickly, her cream filling his mouth, but he wanted more, needed more.

Pulling back his head, he looked up at her. She had a dazed look on her face and her eyes were as dark a green as he'd ever seen them. She moaned when he slid his finger deep inside of her. Sebastian stood up, pulled his pants from his body, and freed his cock. He ached to be inside of her.

She pushed him back against the bed, and he landed on his back. He didn't know what she had planned, but right now he was game for whatever. She told him to get to the middle of the bed, and he scrambled to do as she commanded.

"I want to ride you again. You've no idea how good that feels to be in control of my own body like that." He nodded as she moved up his body, skimming her breast over his cock as she went. "I want you not to touch me until I tell you to. Can you do that?"

"Yes," he responded hoarsely. "I can do that, but I will want the same thing when you're finished with me."

"I'll never be finished with you." He wrapped his hands around the headboard and watched her. His heart was pounding in his chest, and he could hardly catch his breath. She licked his cock, and he felt his balls tighten. She was going to make him come right now if she kept that up. He nearly told her so when she swallowed him.

"Christ." He jerked up from the bed and was glad he'd held onto the headboard. Otherwise, he might have flown up off the bed and onto the ceiling. She moved up over him, and he took her mouth when she brushed against his.

She fisted his cock and lowered herself over him. As he rocked up, she pressed him back down with her weight. Ama moved slowly over him, her hips rolling forward just enough to let him know that her ride was going to last for as long as it took her to kill him. He gripped the bed harder, knowing that if he let go she'd quit.

"I love you." He nodded, unable to speak. "And having your cock in me like this is amazing."

Bending his knees, he used his feet to roll with her. She leaned back against his thighs, and her hand moved down her belly to her pussy. Sebastian watched as her fingers joined his cock inside of her. When she opened her nether lips with her free hand, he could see her clit and that she was careful only to brush against it and not pinch it as he wanted to do.

He was ready to do just that when she scissored her fingers over her clit and squeezed. Her climax rolled from her and over him. As she rode her own hand and his cock, he reached down and pulled her hips over him faster. He needed to come, and he didn't care if she stopped now or not.

Lowering his legs, he sat up and took her nipple into his mouth and bit her. She screamed out his name and he bit again. Blood tangled around his tongue as he sealed the wound, and he rolled her to her back.

"I'm going to fuck you hard, baby. You've taken all my good intentions out of the picture the moment you sucked me down your throat and swallowed me." She nodded and wrapped her legs around his hips. "Mark me baby. Please. I need to feel you make me yours."

He pounded hard into her and felt her nails tear at his skin as she held onto his shoulders. The harder he took her, the harder she met each of his strokes. Nuzzling her neck, he knew that he wasn't going to last long and licked a path from her shoulder to the sweet spot just behind her ear. Her body shuddered beneath his as she sank her teeth into his arm. Christ, his mind exploded along with his body.

Sebastian knew the moment that he sank his teeth into her that he had hurt her. She screamed against his arm, and he started to lift his head when she wrapped her hand into his hair and held him there. Sucking hard on the wound, he took as much of her essences into him as he could and roared as his climax grabbed him by the balls again and felt as if they were being twisted hard. He came again, and this time she roared out her release as he did.

He held her to him as she continued to spasm beneath him. He rolled to his back, never leaving her body, and held her over him. He was just closing his eyes when she spoke. Pulling her tighter, he felt her tears touch his chest.

"I thought you were going to die." She looked up at him, tears staining her cheeks. "I thought for sure that I'd killed you when...you were hurting so badly that I didn't know what do to."

"I thought I was, too, until I realized it wasn't me but Wanera. He thought this would happen, I think, but wasn't sure. I'm glad that we were able to help him...I'm glad that you were able to help him."

"Khan stayed behind and...he won't tell us what happened, but I think he killed that woman who hurt you both. I thought Monica was going to murder him when he came back. But his dad only nodded like he would have done the same thing in his place." Sebastian thought his dad would have, too.

"He didn't kill her, he told me. But I'm pretty sure that she's where she doesn't want to be." He'd had a couple of dreams about her. He was sure that the man, her boss, had shown him that because he wanted him to be sure that she'd never harm them again. "We won't have to worry about her again."

"Good." She stretched out over him and he felt his body respond. "We had a delivery while you were resting. Our...uniforms, I suppose you could call them, arrived for the ball. I'm pretty sure that we're not going to be wearing them out in public ever, but they are sort of pretty."

"Pretty? I'm not fond of that word when it comes to clothing I'm expected to wear. Especially when it's in a public forum." She giggled. "Ama, what is it I should know?"

Her peals of laughter didn't reassure him. Neither did her evasion of the question as the day wore on. By the time they were eating dinner, he decided that he was going to find the box of whatever it was and burn it. Nothing that made her laugh this hard was going to be anything he wanted to have even near his body. He knew this wasn't going to end well.

~~~

The ball was in three hours and she still wasn't even close to being ready. She glanced over at Sebastian as he lounged on the bed, refusing to wear the clothes that had been sent for him. She looked at her own dress and decided that he might be right. They were more suited to a costume party than something as formal as this thing was turning out to be.

The invitations for the family had arrived that morning, as well as instructions on how to dress. Formal was in bold letters and a good half inch wide. It also stated that there was a reception following. Following what, she wasn't sure, and since she'd tossed her father out, she couldn't contact Jacob either. She was as nervous as she'd ever been and eyed the empty glass of tea on the dresser.

"You could simply wear the dress that I picked out for you. It'll make you feel better, because there is no way I'm putting that thing on me and going out." He handed her his glass of tea and kissed her exposed shoulder. "I'm thinking that staying home is sounding better and better all the time."

She agreed and told him so. "I don't even know what to do once we get there, or if I should have made arrangements for the food. What if we get there and there's twenty people and nothing but a bunch of overturned crates for them to sit on and nothing to eat?" He shrugged. "This is serious. This is something that's supposed to be important and we don't have a clue what we're doing."

"Who really cares? I mean really, we're going to a ball neither of us wants to go to, we're supposed to wear those ridiculous clothes that no one explained to us why, and we're not even sure that it's going to be set up. So again, who cares? If we're the only ones that show up, we'll just get back in the car and come back here and make love for the rest of the night." He wiggled his brows at her. "We can go in the woods and have some fun. You're beautiful in the moon light."

She let him hold her as she thought about what he'd said. "What if we just go and stay long enough to make sure that we're not going to be made to look stupid, then come back here and do as you said? I think I can live with that." More than she could making a fool of herself. "I think this is stupid anyway. Who cares that we're some king and queen of a bunch of little pixies anyway?"

Two and a half hours later, she was pulling on the dress that he'd picked out and felt better already. When the car, a large white limo, pulled to a smooth stop in front of their home, she looked at Sebastian again. He kissed her nose and gave her his elbow. His tux looked much better on him than that ridiculous costume had.

It had been made of silk, the only redeeming thing about it, but it had been a bright purple. The sleeves were bejeweled with all manner of sequins and pearls that sparkled around the room like a seventies disco ball. She laughed at him so hard when he'd tried it on that he wouldn't even put on the accompanying hat and pants. She had pulled them out and put them on the bed and fell over laughing at the amount of sequins on the pants. He would have set off alarms in any airport there were so many of them. And the colors were enough to hurt your eyes if he moved suddenly. She smiled when she thought of the hat.

It had been large and velvet. The large feather, a seriously large feather, had hung down from it nearly a foot. She had touched it once, and when it changed to the colors she had on, she jerked back from it so quickly that she fell over the box her dress had come in. It was worse than his suit had been, and she'd yet to pull it even close to her body, much less over it. She slid into the back seat after being handed in by Sebastian.

"That dress is going to look very good lying next to the bed when I tear it from you later." She smiled at him and let her cat purr a little. "You do that much more and we'll never leave this limo. I can't wait much longer to have you naked again."

She smiled. "You and I just made love not an hour ago. Remember? I had to take another shower so I could get the tangles out of my hair.

He nodded. "You screamed my name so hard when you came that I thought you'd break crystal. I love it when you do that."

She looked down at her dress and knew that she'd never worn anything more beautiful. It was a light green silk and clung to her body like it was made over her. She ran her hand along the waist and felt the tiny little flowers that had been stitched into it. She looked up at him when he growled.

"I want you." She shook her head and smiled. "You do know that the longer I wait to have you, the harder I'm going to fuck you when I do."

"I know," she said as the limo stopped moving. "What do you think I'm doing this for? I love to have you pound into me and sink your canines into my shoulder when you come."

The door opened before he could comment. She was glad because when she reached for the drivers hand to help her out, she felt his teeth bite into her ass as she moved. She nearly fell into the other man's arms when she stumbled. When Sebastian got out, she could see that his cat was just as needy as the man. He rolled over Sebastian like a glove, his colors fighting for room over his flesh.

"You're going to pay for that." He whispered in her ear and nipped at her lobe. "You're so going to pay for that."

She was barely paying attention. The building where they'd first met about this thing was transformed. It looked like something out of a fairy land where castles might exist. She looked at Monica and the rest as they came toward them. Each of the men was dressed in the same style of tux as Sebastian, and the women were all dressed in silk and lace. She laughed when she saw George.

He had opted for a bola, not a tie. And his tux was white. She smiled at him when he winked at her. Corrine smacked his arm.

"The old fool had to be different. He just couldn't pick out a black tux. No, he had to be special." Corrine fussed with his lapel and Ama knew that Corrine was very proud of her husband and loved him dearly. "Next time you have one of these shingle dingles, I'm going to make sure he conforms."

"No, you won't." George kissed his mate soundly on the mouth before she could speak again. "You'll let me wear what I want or we'll stay home and I'll chase you around the dining room again."

The boys all groaned, and the rest of them laughed. She loved these two very much, and was glad now that she'd decided to help them with their computer. They were the best thing that had happened to her.

The entrance to the building was lined with guards, each of them wearing the purple of the clothing that had been sent to Ama and Sebastian. They had a moment of panic that they'd not be allowed entrance to their own "shingle dingle," as Corrine had called it. But the moment she and Sebastian stepped on the first step, the guards came to attention and raised their swords to their chin. She looked at Sebastian.

"You ready?" She nodded in response. "Then let's get this over with. I want to get out of this suit and into you as soon as possible."

As soon as they stepped over the threshold, she knew that whatever they wore, everyone in this room would know who they were. And there were a great many people in the room with them. Ama gripped Sebastian to her as they walked past the guard. This was on a grand scale like she'd never seen before.

"Hello." The woman who suddenly appeared before them was dressed in the same purple as the guard. "My name is Peony. I'm from the Ninth Ward and here to make sure you are well received."

"I'm Ama, and this is…." The woman nodded at her and smiled. "You know who we are, don't you?"

"Yes, my lady, we all do. And I must say that I'm glad to see that you are a forward thinking king and queen. When I was asked to send you the attire for this evening, I shuddered to think what you'd do with them. I would have tossed them on the floor and set them to flames." Ama nodded. "Come. Let me introduce you to your host. His name is Lord Galin Derik. He is the prince of my ward."

The night was a blur after the first hour. They were introduced to every person in the room. And once she'd talked with Lord Galin, the rest of the people in the room seemed to relax. As they ate the bounty on the laden tables and drank juice for hours, she began to see that this was just what the lord had told her it was…a way for everyone to meet them.

"I had hoped that your sire would be here, but he has…I believe he said he had other plans." She had smiled at Lord Galin. "The man is a fool if he thought that he could run you like he did his mate. There was not a more stubborn man than him, and he never let up."

"You knew my mother then?" Galin nodded. "I didn't know her before she thought my father died. But she was broken. I don't think she would have lived had it not been for me."

"You're correct. There was not a woman who loved her mate as she did him." He smiled. "Except for the way you love yours. You two are very much in love."

"We are." She looked for Sebastian across the room, and he turned to her just as she thought of him. "He makes me feel like I can take on the world and win."

"As it should be." Galin took her to the gifts that had been brought. "Most of these you will find useless. There are some things among them that you could and probably should put to the trash bin. But the books…there are four of them you should read. They will help you in your days to come."

"And where will we be in the days that come?" He grinned at her again. "I don't want to leave my family. I've only just found them and I want to keep them close to me."

"You can stay where you are. No one need have you in their realms unless there is a problem. And as I've been watching them for you, it has been smooth riding. Actually, I'm sad to give it over to you. I wish only my own realm ran so well."

"So we just watch over the realms and do what it needs to keep them running." He told her pretty much that was it. "I don't understand what the deal is then. I mean, if it runs so well with you, why do they need me?"

"Because you're their queen. It is as it's always been." He bowed before her. "You will be fine, my lady. Simply do what you do best and things will work out."

She hoped so as they made their way back home. She certainly hoped so. She was ready to begin her life with Sebastian and maybe have a few children. She leaned back against Sebastian's shoulder as they rode home.

"I love you." He held her tighter. "When we get home, I'd very much like to hear about having a baby with you and this going into heat thing."

He laughed. "We might have to practice a great deal before we get it right. The baby making part, I mean."

She didn't care so long as she could practice with him. Closing her eyes, she thought about little boys that looked just like their daddy, and little girls with long blonde hair. Ama knew that they would probably look nothing like she thought, but she didn't care. She would be happy simply to have someone she would be proud to raise. And a mate to do it with.

Life was good.

About the Author

Kathi Barton, author of the bestselling series Force of Nature, lives in Nashport, Ohio with her husband Paul. In addition to writing full time Kathi likes to spend time with her eight grandkids, three children and three children-in-laws. She writes to relax and have fun.

Her muse, a cross between Jimmy Stewart and Hugh Jackman brings them to life for her readers in a way that has them coming back time and again for more. Her favorite genre is paranormal romance with a great deal of spice. You can visit Kathi on line and drop her an email if you'd like. She loves hearing from her fans. aaronskiss@gmail.com.

Follow Kathi on her blog:
http://kathisbartonauthor.blogspot.com/

www.ingramcontent.com/pod-product-compliance
Lightning Source LLC
Chambersburg PA
CBHW021957190626
46808CB00017B/2114